P9-CEB-114

# THE RISK OF GETTING INVOLVED

In the darkness, and long after the other three had sacked out, Theo stared at the ceiling and thought of Pete Duffy and the murder he committed. On the one hand, he was thrilled to be involved in his capture. But, on the other, he was terrified over what it could mean. Pete Duffy had some dangerous friends, and they were still hanging around Strattenburg.

If it was indeed Pete Duffy, and if they caught him and hauled him back for another trial, Theo would not want his name mentioned.

Ike? He wouldn't care. Ike had survived three years in prison. He feared nothing.

## AVAILABLE FROM JOHN GRISHAM

*Theodore Boone: Kid Lawyer*

*Theodore Boone: The Abduction*

*Theodore Boone: The Accused*

*Theodore Boone: The Activist*

*Theodore Boone: The Fugitive*

*Theodore Boone: The Scandal*

# JOHN GRISHAM

# THEODORE the fugitive BOONE

PUFFIN BOOKS

PUFFIN BOOKS

An imprint of Penguin Random House LLC

375 Hudson Street

New York, New York 10014

First published in the United States of America by Dutton Children's Books,

a division of Penguin Young Readers Group, 2015

Published by Puffin Books, an imprint of Penguin Random House LLC, 2016

Copyright © 2015 by Boone & Boone LLC

Penguin supports copyright. Copyright fuels creativity, encourages diverse voices, promotes free speech, and creates a vibrant culture. Thank you for buying an authorized edition of this book and for complying with copyright laws by not reproducing, scanning, or distributing any part of it in any form without permission. You are supporting writers and allowing Penguin to continue to publish books for every reader.

LIBRARY OF CONGRESS CATALOGING-IN-PUBLICATION DATA AVAILABLE.

Puffin Books ISBN 9780147510181

Printed in the United States of America

7 9 10 8 6

# THEODORE BOONE
## the fugitive

# PART ONE

## THE CAPTURE

# Chapter 1

Though the streetlights of Strattenburg were still on, and there was no hint of sunlight in the east, the parking lot in front of the middle school was buzzing with energy as almost 175 eighth graders arrived in family cars and vans, all driven by sleepy parents eager to get rid of the kids for a few days. The kids had slept little. They had packed all night, tossed and turned in their beds, hopped out long before sunrise, showered, packed some more, awakened their parents, pushed for a quick breakfast, and in general acted as hyper as a bunch of five-year-olds waiting for Santa. At six a.m., as instructed, they all arrived at the school at the same time. They were greeted by the awesome sight of four long, sleek, matching tour buses in perfect single file with running lights glittering in the dark and diesel engines purring.

The Eighth-Grade Field Trip! Six hours by bus to Washington, DC, for three-and-a-half days of seeing the sights and four nights of mischief in a high-rise hotel. For this, the students had worked for months—selling doughnuts on Saturday mornings, washing a thousand cars, cleaning roadside ditches and recycling the aluminum cans, soliciting the same downtown merchants who contributed every year, selling fruitcakes door-to-door at Christmas, auctioning used sports equipment, holding bake-a-thons and bike-a-thons and book-a-thons, and pursuing with enthusiasm any number of mildly profitable ventures approved by the Field Trip Committee. All proceeds went into the same pot. The goal had been ten thousand dollars, certainly not enough to cover all expenses but enough to guarantee the trip. This year the class had raised almost twelve thousand dollars, which meant that each student was assessed $125.

There were a few students who could not afford this. However, the school had a long tradition of making sure no one was left behind. Every single eighth grader was headed to Washington, along with ten teachers and eight parents.

Theodore Boone was thrilled that his mother had not volunteered for the trip. They had discussed it over dinner. His father had quickly bowed out, claiming, as usual, that he simply had too much work. Theo's mother, at first, seemed interested in tagging along, but soon realized she could not. Theo checked her trial calendar at the office and knew full well she would be in court while he was having a ball in Washington.

As they waited in traffic, Theo sat in the front seat and stroked the head of his dog, Judge, who was sitting partially on the console and partially in Theo's lap. Judge usually sat wherever he wanted, and none of the Boones told him otherwise.

"Are you excited?" Mr. Boone asked. He had drop-off duty because Mrs. Boone had gone back to bed for another hour of sleep.

"Sure," Theo said, trying to hide his excitement. "A long bus ride, though."

"I'm sure you guys'll be asleep before you get out of town. We've gone over the rules. Any questions?"

"We've been through this a dozen times," Theo said, mildly frustrated. He liked his parents. They were a bit older than average, and he was an only child, and at times they seemed a little too protective. One of the few things that irritated Theo about them was their fondness of rules. All rules, regardless of who made them, must be followed perfectly.

Theo suspected this was because they were both lawyers.

"I know, I know," his father said. "Just follow the rules,

do what your teachers tell you, and don't do anything stupid. Remember what happened two years ago?"

How could Theo, or any other eighth grader, ever forget what happened two years ago? Two bozos—Jimbo Nance and Duck DeFoe—dropped water balloons from a fifth-floor hotel room into the indoor lobby far below. No one was hurt, but some folks got really wet, and really mad. A snitch turned them in, and the boys' parents had to drive six hours in the middle of the night to retrieve them. Then six hours back to Strattenburg. Jimbo said it was a very long drive. They were suspended from classes for a week, and the school was told to find another hotel for future field trips. This misadventure was now legendary around town, and it was used to caution and frighten Theo and every other eighth grader headed to Washington.

They finally parked. Theo said good-bye to Judge and told him to stay in the front seat. Mr. Boone opened a rear door and removed Theo's luggage—one nylon overnight bag that was supposed to weigh under twenty pounds. Anything over twenty pounds would be left behind (one of the Big Rules!), and the guilty kid would be forced to make the trip without the benefit of clean clothes and a toothbrush. This would not have bothered Theo in the least. He had survived a week in the woods with the Boy Scouts with less equipment.

-------

Mr. Mount was standing by a bus with some scales, weighing other luggage as it was loaded into storage. He was smiling and laughing, as excited as his students. Theo's bag weighed nineteen pounds, eight ounces. His backpack barely made the limit at twelve pounds, and Theo was in business. Mr. Mount checked the overnight bag for an ID card and told Theo to get on the bus.

Theo shook his father's hand, said good-bye, froze for a moment, terrified his father might try to hug him or something awful like that, then breathed a sigh of relief when Mr. Boone said, "Have fun. Call your mother." Theo scampered aboard.

Close by, the girls were saying good-bye to their mothers with all manner of embracing, blubbering, and carrying on as if they were going off to war and would probably never come home. By the boys' buses, though, the tough guys stiffened and tried to get away quickly from their parents with as little contact as possible.

The parking lot slowly cleared as the sun rose. At precisely seven a.m., the four buses rolled away from the school. It was Thursday. The big day had finally arrived, and the kids were noisy and rowdy. His seatmate was Chase Whipple, a close friend who was often referred to as "The Mad Scientist." To prevent them from getting lost and wandering through the dangerous streets of DC, the teachers had implemented the Buddy System. For the next four days Theo would be stuck with Chase, and Chase with Theo, and each was supposed to know what the other was doing at all times. Theo knew he got the bad end of the deal because Chase often got lost on the campus of the Strattenburg Middle School. Keeping an eye on him would take some work. They would share a room with Woody Lambert and Aaron Nyquist.

As the buses eased through the quiet streets, the boys chattered excitedly. No one had yet thrown a punch or yanked off someone else's cap. They had been threatened about misbehaving, and Mr. Mount was watching them closely. Then someone behind Theo passed gas, and loudly. This was instantly contagious, and before they were out of Strattenburg Theo wished he could have been sitting with April Finnemore on the other bus just ahead.

Mr. Mount cracked a window. Things eventually settled down. Thirty minutes into the trip, the boys were either asleep or lost in video games.

# Chapter 2

Theo's room was on the eighth floor of a new hotel on Connecticut Avenue, about a half mile north of the White House. From his window, he, along with Chase, Woody, and Aaron, had a clear view of the top half of the Washington Monument rising above the city. According to their schedule, the boys would climb to the top of the monument first thing Saturday morning. But for now, they had to hurry downstairs for a quick lunch, then, they would be off to see the sights.

Each student was allowed to pick and choose from the many attractions in Washington. It would take a year of serious work to see everything, so Mr. Mount and the other teachers had put together a list from which the students could select their favorites.

April had convinced Theo that they should see Ford's Theatre, the place where Abraham Lincoln was shot, and this seemed like an interesting idea. Theo convinced Chase, and after lunch they gathered in the hotel lobby with Mr. Babcock, a history teacher, and a group of eighteen students. Mr. Babcock explained that they would not be taking one of the buses because their group was small. Rather, they would get to experience the DC subway system, known as the Metro. He asked how many of the students had ever ridden on a subway. Theo and three others raised their hands.

They left the hotel and began walking along a busy sidewalk. For kids who lived in a small town, the sounds and energy of a big city were at first hard to absorb. So many big buildings, so many cars bumper to bumper in traffic that hardly moved, so many people bustling along the sidewalks, all anxious to get somewhere. At the Woodley Park Metro Station, they rode the escalator down, far below the streets. Mr. Babcock had plastic SmarTrip cards that would give the students limited use of the Metro system. Their train was half-empty, clean, and efficient. As it zipped along the dark tunnel, April whispered to Theo that it was her first time on a subway. Theo said he'd been on one before in New York, when his parents took him there on vacation. The New York system, though, was far different from DC's.

When the train stopped for the third time, just minutes

after they had started, it was time to get off at the Metro Center Station. They hurried up the steps and back into the sunlight. Mr. Babcock counted eighteen kids, and they began walking. Minutes later they were on 10th Street.

Mr. Babcock stopped the group and pointed across the street to a handsome redbrick building that was obviously important. He said, "That's Ford's Theatre, the place where President Lincoln was shot on April 14, 1865. As you know, because you all have spent so much time doing your history assignments, the Civil War had just ended; in fact, General Lee had surrendered to General Grant only five days earlier at Appomattox Court House in Virginia. The city of Washington was in a good mood, the war was finally over, and so President and Mrs. Lincoln decided to have a night out on the town. Ford's Theatre was the grandest, most magnificent theatre in town, and the Lincolns came here often for concerts and plays. At the time, the theatre had over two thousand seats, and the play, one called *Our American Cousin*, was selling out every night."

They walked half a block and stopped again. Mr. Babcock resumed with, "Now, the war may have been over, but a lot of folks didn't think so. One was a Confederate named John Wilkes Booth. He was a well-known actor, and he was even photographed with President Lincoln during his second inauguration, a month earlier. Mr. Booth was upset because the South had surrendered, and he was desperate to do something to help its cause. So he decided to kill President Lincoln. Because he was known to the theatre personnel, he was allowed to approach the box where the Lincolns were sitting. He shot the president once in the back of the head, jumped onto the stage, broke his leg, then, escaped out the back door."

Mr. Babcock turned and nodded at the building beside them. He said, "This is the Petersen House, which at that time was a boardinghouse. They brought President Lincoln over here, where he was attended to by his doctors throughout the night. Word spread quickly. A crowd gathered, and federal troops were used to keep people away from the house. President Lincoln died here on the morning of April 15, 1865."

Enough of the lecture. They finally crossed the street and entered Ford's Theatre.

After two hours, Theo had had enough of the Lincoln killing. It was certainly interesting and all that, and he appreciated the historical importance, but it was time to move on. The coolest thing was down in the museum, under the stage, where they displayed the actual gun Booth used.

It was almost four thirty when they emerged onto 10th Street and headed back to the Metro Center Station. The traffic was even heavier, the sidewalks more crowded. Their train was packed with commuters headed home and seemed to move a lot slower. Theo was standing in the middle of the car, in a crowd, with Chase and April close by, as the train rocked and clicked along the tracks. He glanced around him at the glum faces of the commuters; no one was smiling. They all looked tired. He wasn't sure where he would live when he grew up, but he didn't think it would be in a big city. Strattenburg seemed the perfect size. Not too big, not too small. No traffic jams. No angry horn blowing. No crowded sidewalks. He didn't want to ride a train to and from work.

A man seated tightly between two women lowered his newspaper as he flipped a page. He was less than ten feet away from Theo.

He looked familiar, oddly familiar. Theo took a deep breath and managed to wiggle between two men bunched together with the others. A few feet closer now, and he could see the man's face.

He'd seen it before, but where? There was something different about it, maybe the hair was darker, maybe the reading glasses were new. Suddenly, it struck Theo like a brick against the head: The face belonged to Pete Duffy.

Pete Duffy? The most wanted man in the history of Strattenburg and Stratten County. Number seven on the FBI's Ten Most Wanted. The man who'd been accused of murdering his wife, had gone to trial in Strattenburg, in front of Judge Henry Gantry, a trial that Theo and his classmates had actually watched. The man who'd barely escaped a conviction when Judge Gantry declared a mistrial. The man who'd fled town in the middle of the night and had not been heard from since.

The man lowered the newspaper again as he flipped another page. He glanced around as Theo ducked behind another commuter. They had exchanged stares just after the trial.

Duffy had a mustache now, one sprinkled with gray whiskers. His face disappeared again behind the newspaper.

Theo was paralyzed with uncertainty. He had no idea what to do. The train stopped and more commuters piled on. It stopped again at the Dupont Circle Station. The Woodley Park Station was next. Duffy showed no signs of getting off. He did not appear to have a briefcase or bag or satchel like the other commuters. Theo squirmed his way down the train, putting a few more feet between himself and his classmates. Chase was lost in another world, as usual. April could not be seen. He could hear Mr. Babcock tell the students to get ready to get off. Theo moved farther away.

At the Woodley Park Station, the train stopped and the doors flew open. More commuters rushed on as the students scrambled to get off. In the melee, no one noticed that Theo was still on the train. The doors closed and it took off again. He kept his eyes on Pete Duffy, who was ducking behind the newspaper, probably a habit now. At the Cleveland Park Station, a few more passengers got on. Theo sent a text message to Chase explaining that he had been unable to get off, and that he was okay. He'd simply catch another train back to Woodley Park. Chase called immediately but Theo kept his phone on mute. He was sure Mr. Babcock was panicked. He would return the call in just a few minutes.

Theo began toying with his cell phone, as if he might be sending texts or playing games. He had the camera on, the video, and he was scanning the car, just another goofy thirteen-year-old being rude with a phone. Pete Duffy was fifteen feet away, sitting calmly behind his newspaper. Theo waited and waited. Finally, as the train approached the Tenleytown Station, Duffy lowered the paper and folded it.

He stuck it under his arm, and for about five seconds Theo nailed him with the video. He even managed to zoom closer. When Duffy looked his way, Theo giggled at his camera as if he'd scored points in a game.

At the Tenleytown Station, Duffy got off the train, and Theo followed him. Duffy walked quickly, as if he lived with the fear of being followed. After a few minutes, Theo lost him in a crowd. He called Chase, said he was waiting on the next train, and should be there in fifteen minutes.

# Chapter 3

M r. Babcock was waiting at the Woodley Park Station, and he was not happy. Theo apologized repeatedly, fibbing that he had been caught in the crush of people and simply could not get off the train in time. Theo did not like the fact that he was being forced to lie. It was wrong and he tried to tell the truth at all times. However, occasionally he found himself in the awkward position of having to fudge on the truth for a good reason. On the subway, he had made the quick decision that it was more important to try and nail Pete Duffy than to get off when and where he was supposed to. If he got off with his classmates, Duffy would be gone, and a great chance to nail him would have been missed. Now, if he admitted to Mr. Babcock that he had deliberately stayed on the train, then all sorts of bad stuff would happen. He could not tell the truth about Pete Duffy, not now anyway, because he had no idea what to do with the truth. He needed some time alone to think things through.

He needed to talk to Uncle Ike.

For the moment, though, he was forced to apologize to Mr. Babcock, who was a nervous type to begin with. Back at the hotel, Mr. Babcock marched Theo over to Mr. Mount and made a full report of his student's misdeed. As soon as Mr. Babcock walked away, Theo mumbled, "That guy just needs to relax."

Mr. Mount, who trusted Theo and knew that if any kid could survive in the big city it was Theodore Boone, agreed and said, "Don't do it again, okay? Just pay attention to where you are."

"Sure," Theo said. *If you only knew.*

Dinner was a pizza party in a hotel ballroom. Seating was not regulated; you could sit anywhere you wanted. So, typically, the boys took one side of the room and the girls the other. Theo nibbled on some crust and sipped water from a bottle, but his mind was not on pizza. He was certain he had seen Pete Duffy. He even remembered the way the man walked as he was entering and leaving the courthouse during his trial. It was the same walk. The same height and body type. Definitely the same eyes, nose, forehead, and chin. Theo had locked himself in his hotel bathroom and watched the video on his phone a dozen times.

Theo had found Pete Duffy! He still couldn't believe it and he was still uncertain about what to do next, but in his excitement he had almost forgotten something important. Since Duffy had fled town, the police had posted a $100,000 reward for information leading to his arrest and conviction. In his room before dinner, Theo had gone online and verified this reward. The Strattenburg police website had several pages dedicated to the Duffy case. There were several close-up photos of his face.

Cell phones were strictly prohibited during meals—if one was seen by an adult it was to be immediately confiscated. Halfway through the pizza party, Theo informed Mr. Mount that he needed to walk down the hallway to the restroom. Once inside, Theo locked himself in a stall and called Ike.

"I thought you were in Washington," Ike said.

"I am. Ike, I saw Pete Duffy on the Metro. I know it's him."

"I thought he was in Cambodia or some place."

"Not now. He's right here in Washington. I got him on video. I'll e-mail it to you right now. Take a look and I'll call you later."

"You're serious, aren't you?" Ike said, his voice suddenly sharper.

"Dead serious. Later." Theo quickly e-mailed the video to Ike, then left the restroom and hustled back to the ballroom.

After dinner, when it was dark, the entire eighth grade loaded onto the four buses and headed for the Lincoln Memorial. There, they milled about the famous statue of Lincoln sitting and staring seriously—*did the guy ever smile?* Theo wondered—while clutching the sides of his chair. The lights cast even more shadows on his face, and Theo found it all quite awesome. With the assistance of a park ranger, Mr. Babcock, who evidently was a big Lincoln fan, set up a large screen at the foot of the steps—fifty-eight steps to be exact—and the students gathered around for a quick lecture. They listened in perfect silence as Mr. Babcock recapped the significant events of Lincoln's life, material they had all covered in class, which now meant much more sitting on the steps of his memorial. As he spoke, Mr. Babcock, who was a compelling teacher, flashed photos of Lincoln as he advanced through his life.

Though the students were sitting on marble steps, there was no wiggling and no whispering. They absorbed the lecture with great interest. When Theo looked away, he gazed upon the awesome sight of the Reflecting Pool just in front of them. Beyond it, a mile away, was the towering Washington Monument, also lit to perfection. And beyond that, another mile away, was the US Capitol, its dome glowing magnificently in the night. When Theo turned around, he found President Lincoln staring down at them.

Theo knew it was a moment he would never forget.

They gave Mr. Babcock a round of applause when he finished. Next up was Ms. Greenwood, a popular African American lady who taught English to the girls. She began by asking the students to look all the way down to the Washington Monument and to try to imagine the Mall packed with almost a quarter of a million people. The day was August 28, 1963, and black people from all over America had marched on Washington to demand justice and equality. They were led by a young Baptist minister from Atlanta named Dr. Martin Luther King Jr.

As she spoke, she flashed images onto the screen, photos of the crowd that day, of people marching and carrying signs. She explained that Dr. King delivered one of the most famous speeches in American history, right over there on a temporary podium, under the proud gaze of the president who ended slavery. She then played a tape of the speech, black-and-white footage of Dr. King and his dream.

Theo had seen and heard the speech before, but it was far more moving at that moment. As Dr. King's words echoed through the night, Theo looked down the Mall and tried to imagine what it was like that day, with thousands of people packed together and listening to words that would live forever.

They applauded for Ms. Greenwood, too, when she finished. Mr. Mount said there would be no more lectures. The students were allowed to hang around the Reflecting Pool for an hour or so. Theo found a seat on a park bench and texted Ike: *Did you get video? What do you think?*

Evidently, Ike was waiting: *I'd say it's p duffy. Let's talk. Okay. Later.*

Later, at the hotel, as his three roommates were watching television and waiting on the 'lights-out' order from Mr. Mount, Theo went to the bathroom, locked the door, and took a seat on the toilet. He called Ike, who again seemed to be waiting with the phone in his hand. He asked, "Have you told anyone?"

"Of course not," Theo said. "No one but you. What are we going to do?"

"I've been thinking and I have a plan. I'll catch an early flight to DC and land at National around noon. I want to be on the subway when he gets on this afternoon and follow him as closely as I can. I need the time, the station, and the Metro line."

Theo had already taken notes and had it memorized. "It's the Red Line. We got on at the Metro Center Station, and I'm positive he was already on the train."

"How many cars on the train?"

"Uh, just guessing, I would say seven or eight."

"And which car did you get in?"

"Don't know, but somewhere close to the middle."

"What time was it?"

"Somewhere between four thirty and five. He stayed on the Red Line and got off at the Tenleytown Station. I followed him for about three blocks before I lost him. I didn't want to get too far from the station; not exactly my neck of the woods, you know."

"Okay, that's all I need. I'll be there tomorrow. I'm assuming you're tied up all day."

"All day and all night. We're doing the Smithsonian tomorrow."

"Have fun. I'll text you tomorrow night."

Theo was relieved to have an adult involved, even if the adult was Uncle Ike. He was worried, though, about the old guy's appearance. Ike was in his mid-sixties and not aging that well. He wore his white hair long and tied in a ponytail. He had a scraggly gray beard, and usually wore funky T-shirts, battered old jeans, weird eyeglasses, and sandals, even in cold weather. All in all, Ike Boone was the kind of person who attracts more attention than deflects it. He tended to keep to himself, but he was still known around town. If Pete Duffy had ever met Ike, or seen him, there was a good chance he would remember him. Surely Ike would go heavy on the disguises.

In the darkness, and long after the other three had sacked out, Theo stared at the ceiling and thought of Pete Duffy and the murder he committed. On the one hand, he was thrilled to be involved in his capture. But, on the other, he was terrified over what it could mean. Pete Duffy had some dangerous friends, and they were still hanging around Strattenburg.

If it was indeed Pete Duffy, and if they caught him and hauled him back for another trial, Theo would not want his name mentioned.

Ike? He wouldn't care. Ike had survived three years in prison. He feared nothing.

# Chapter 4

At nine a.m. Friday, the four buses from Strattenburg pulled up to the east entrance of the Smithsonian Institution and all the eighth graders spilled out. The Smithsonian is the largest museum in the world, and a person could spend a week there and not see everything. In planning the day, Mr. Mount had explained to his class that the Smithsonian is actually a group of nineteen different museums and a zoo, along with a bunch of collections and galleries, and eleven of the nineteen are located on the Mall. It is home to about 138 million items, everything imaginable, and is nicknamed the "nation's attic." Thirty million people each year visit the Smithsonian.

The students divided into groups. Theo and about forty others headed for the National Air and Space Museum.

They spent two hours there, then regrouped and headed for the National Museum of American History.

At two thirty, Theo received a text from Ike that read: *In town, about to check out the Metro system.* Theo was tired of museums and wished he could sneak away and do detective work with Ike. By five p.m., he felt as though he had seen at least 100 million items and needed a break. They boarded the buses and returned to the hotel for dinner.

At six forty-five, while Theo was resting in his room and watching television, he received another text from Ike: *Downstairs in lobby. Can u come down?*

Theo replied: *Sure.* He told Chase, Woody, and Aaron that his uncle had stopped by the hotel and wanted to say hello. Minutes later, he was walking through the lobby and couldn't find Ike. Finally, a man sitting in a coffee bar waved at him, and Theo realized it was his uncle. Dark suit, brown leather shoes, white shirt, no tie, and some type of beret on his head that covered most of his white hair. The rest, the long part, was stuffed under his collar. Theo would never have recognized him.

Ike was sipping coffee and smiling at his favorite nephew. "So how's the great tour of Washington going?" he asked.

Theo gave a heavy sigh as if he were exhausted. He rattled off the adventures of the day at the Smithsonian, and said, "Tonight, we're watching a documentary film at the Newseum. Tomorrow we do the Washington Monument, and then visit the war memorials. Sunday, we see the Capitol, the White House, and the Jefferson Memorial, and by Monday I think I'll be ready to head home."

"But you're having fun, right?"

"Sure, a lot of fun. Ford's Theatre was pretty cool. So was the Lincoln Memorial. Did you see Pete Duffy?"

"Are you going to the Vietnam Veterans Memorial?"

"Yes, it's on the schedule."

"Well, when you get there, look for the name of Joel Furniss. We grew up together and finished high school at the same time. He was the first boy from Stratten County to be killed in Vietnam, in 1965. There were four others, and their names are on the monument outside our courthouse. You've probably seen it."

"I have. I see it all the time. We studied that war in history, and, I gotta say, I really don't understand it."

"Well, neither did we. It was a national tragedy." Ike took a sip of coffee and seemed to gaze far away for a moment.

"Did you see Pete Duffy?" Theo asked.

"Oh yes," Ike said, snapping back and glancing around,

as if the wrong people might be listening. No one was sitting within thirty feet. Theo glanced into the wide, open lobby and saw Mr. Mount walk through in the distance.

Ike continued, "I camped out in the Judiciary Square Station, two stops before Metro Center, where you guys got on yesterday. I saw no one who looked familiar. The train arrived at four forty-five. Eight cars. I got in number three, looked around as quickly as possible, did not see anyone. At the Metro Center stop, I moved to the fourth car. No one. At the Farragut North Station, I moved to the fifth car, and, bingo. It was crowded, as you said, and I slowly moved closer to the man we're calling Pete Duffy. He was lost behind his newspaper, but I could see the side of his face. He never looked up, never looked around, he was lost in his own world. I backed away and stayed hidden in the crowd. As we approached the Tenleytown Station, he folded his newspaper and stood up. When the train stopped, he got off. I tagged along and was able to follow him to a small apartment building on Forty-Fourth Street. He ducked inside. I assume that's where he's hiding."

"Why would he hide in Washington? Why not Mexico or Australia?"

"Because that's where we expect him to be. Often, it's the guy who's hiding in plain sight that's never discovered."

"I saw a movie one time where this guy was running from the FBI, and he had all kinds of plastic surgery to redo his face. You think Duffy's done that?"

"No, but he's definitely changed hair color and grown a mustache. He's wearing glasses, but they're fake. I watched him read the newspaper, and he did so while looking over his glasses."

"So why is he here?"

"Don't know, but he could be waiting on a fresh set of papers—driver's license, birth certificate, Social Security card, passport. There are a lot of good forgers here in DC, shady outfits that can produce all manner of paperwork that looks legitimate. It's not easy leaving the country on the run, and it can be even harder entering another country without good paperwork. Also, maybe he's staying close to his money. Maybe he has a friend or two here and they're helping him plan his escape. I don't know, Theo, but I'll bet he's not staying here for long."

"Okay, Uncle Ike, you're the adult. What's the plan?"

"Well, we have to move fast. My flight doesn't leave until noon tomorrow, so I'm thinking about getting up early and getting back on the train. I'll try and pick him up at the Tenleytown Station and follow him in, try and see where he goes during the day. I'm going to be very careful because if he gets suspicious he'll just vanish again. Then I'll hop on the plane and be back in Strattenburg tomorrow night. Have you ever heard of some software called FuzziFace?"

"No. What is it?"

"You download it, costs about a hundred bucks, and you match up photographs of faces to identify whoever you're looking for. I'll find an old photo of Pete Duffy, probably one from the newspaper's archives, and try to match it with a still shot from your video. If it nails him, the next step is to go to the police. I play poker every Thursday night with a retired detective named Slats Stillman, an old guy who's still in thick with the police chief. I'm thinking of running it by Slats and getting his advice. I figure the police will move quick. With some luck, they'll have Duffy in custody in a matter of days. They'll hustle him back to Strattenburg for another trial."

"A big trial, right?"

"Just like the last one, only Duffy will also face charges of taking flight and being a fugitive. His goose is cooked, Theo, and you're the hero."

"I don't want to be the hero, Ike. I keep thinking about Omar Cheepe and Paco and those other tough guys who work for Pete Duffy. I'm sure they're still around. I don't want my name mentioned."

"I'm sure we can keep things quiet."

"And if there's a big trial, that means Bobby Escobar will have to testify."

"Of course it does. He's the star witness. He's still in town, right?"

"I think so, but . . . the last time I talked to Julio they were all living in the same apartment, still waiting on immigration documents."

"Does Bobby still work at the golf course?"

"I think so. This worries me, Ike."

"Look, Theo, I'm sure the police will be very careful in dealing with Bobby Escobar. The prosecution's case is pretty weak without him, and the police will protect him. We can't allow thugs to influence our judicial system. Come on, you're a lawyer, you know how important it is to have fair trials. Judge Gantry will be in charge, and if he gets wind of any type of threats made to a witness, he'll lower the boom on Duffy and his gang. It's time to step up."

Theo suspected that Ike's eagerness to nail Duffy and to protect the idea of fair trials also had something to do with the reward money: $100,000.

Theo said, "I need to go. Be careful tomorrow."

"I'm not getting caught, Theo. You didn't recognize me, did you?"

"No, and you look nice for a change, almost like a real lawyer."

"Gee, thanks. And I have another disguise for tomorrow, then, it's back to the old wardrobe."

"Thanks for coming, Ike."

"I wouldn't miss it for the world. I haven't had this much excitement since I got out of prison."

"See you later."

"You take care and have some fun. And, Theo, nice work."

As Theo rode the elevator back to his room, he asked himself if he was doing the right thing. Bringing a murderer to justice sounded great, but there could be a price to pay. He thought about calling his parents and telling them, but such a call would only worry them. He was supposed to be in Washington having a ball as a tourist, not playing detective and stalking a killer.

He trusted his uncle. Ike always knew what to do.

Early Saturday morning, Theo, his roommates, and forty other students got off the bus near the Mall and headed toward the Washington Monument. As they got closer to it, Mr. Mount began a walking tour. He explained that the monument, built of course to honor our first president, is a true obelisk and is constructed of marble and granite.

At 555 feet in height it is still the world's tallest all-stone obelisk. When it was completed in 1884, it was the tallest structure in the world, a record it held until 1889 when the Eiffel Tower was finished in Paris. Construction was started in 1848, and it took six years to build the first 150 feet. Then, for a number of reasons, including a shortage of money and the Civil War, work on the monument was halted for twenty-three years.

Theo wasn't sure about the other students, but after two days of nonstop history lessons, the dates and numbers were beginning to run together.

They gathered at the base of the monument, waited in line for almost an hour, then entered the ground floor lobby. A friendly park ranger guided them to an elevator and locked the door. Seventy seconds later, they stepped out and onto an observation deck five hundred feet above the ground. The views were stunning. To the west were the Reflecting Pool and the Lincoln Memorial. To the north were The Ellipse and the White House. To the east was the magnificent US Capitol. To the southeast were the Smithsonian and rows of government buildings. Below the observation deck was a museum filled with even more history.

After two long hours, the students were ready to move

on. They descended in the elevator and left the lobby.

At eleven forty-six, Theo got a text from Ike: *No sign of Duffy. Must have different routine for Sat. At airport, headed home. C U there.*

# Chapter 5

Mrs. Boone picked Theo up at the school Monday afternoon. During the ten-minute drive home, she wanted to know every detail about the trip and Washington. Theo was tired—he had slept little Sunday night because Woody and Aaron played a stupid game to see which one could stay awake until morning, and he hadn't slept on the bus because there had been a lot of punching, slapping, loud music, laughing, and, of course, passing of gas—so he had little to say to his mother. He promised her he would give her a full report after a nap. At home, she fixed him a grilled cheese sandwich and asked him when was the last time he took a shower. He thought it was either Friday or Saturday, and she instructed him to take one right then, after lunch. When Theo was in the shower, she went back to the office.

Theo Boone did not take naps. Even though he was dead tired, he had somewhere to go. It was, after all, Monday afternoon and he was required to visit Ike. He did not always look forward to these visits, but today was different. They had important business.

Ike had been able to run a number of photos of Pete Duffy through FuzziFace, and Theo was eager to know what he had found.

It was the old Ike—no dark suit, no white shirt and tie, no shiny leather loafers. Instead, he was wearing his standard office attire of faded jeans, faded T-shirt, and sandals. Bob Dylan was singing softly on the stereo when Theo and Judge bounded up the stairs to his messy office. Ike was excited and spent fifteen minutes showing Theo the various images of Pete Duffy on his laptop. The FuzziFace software analyzed every inch of Duffy's face from the old photos Ike had found, and compared those to a still shot from Theo's video. The bottom line: There was an 85 percent chance it was Duffy.

Theo and Ike were convinced beyond a doubt.

"Now what?" Theo asked.

"Have you told your parents?"

"No, but we should. I don't like keeping secrets from them, especially something as big as this. They might even be ticked off when we tell them everything we've already done."

"Okay, I agree. When do you want to tell them?"

"How about now? They're both in the office. It's Monday, so we'll go to Robilio's for dinner, as always. Let's catch them in about half an hour. Will you come with me?"

It was a complicated question because Ike avoided the law offices of Boone & Boone. He had once worked there; in fact, he and Theo's father had started the first Boone law firm in the same building many years earlier. Then something bad happened. Ike got into trouble, left the firm on bad terms, lost his license to practice law, went to prison, and now generally avoided anything to do with his old firm. But, thanks to Theo, the difficult relationship between Ike and Woods Boone was showing signs of improving. During the first Duffy trial, Ike showed up at the office one night when Judge Gantry stopped by for an important conversation with the entire family.

Ike would do almost anything for his nephew. "Sure," he said. "Let's go."

"Great. I'll see you there." Theo and Judge left in a hurry. After four days in the big city, Theo was thrilled to be back on his bike and darting along the streets of Strattenburg. These were his streets and he knew every one of them, and every alley and shortcut. He could not imagine being a kid in a big city where the streets were clogged with cars and the sidewalks were packed with pedestrians.

Theo took the long way back to the office, stalling until five thirty when Elsa Miller would close up her desk, lock the front door, and go home. Elsa was the firm's receptionist and head secretary, and a very important person in the lives of the Boones. She was like a grandmother to Theo, and at that moment she would pounce on him with amazing energy, even more amazing when you considered that she was seventy years old, and hit him with a hundred questions about his trip to Washington. Theo just wasn't in the mood, so he did a few laps around the block, with Judge close behind. He hid behind a tree down the street—a favorite hiding place—until he saw Elsa's car leave. He entered the building through a rear door and went straight to his mother's office. As usual, she was on the phone. Judge parked himself on a dog bed by Elsa's desk, one of three such beds at the office, while Theo went up the stairs to check on his father.

Woods Boone was smoking his pipe and reading a document. His desk was stacked with papers and files, many of them untouched for months, maybe even years. He smiled when he saw Theo and said, "Well, well, how was the big trip?"

"It was great, Dad. I'll tell you all about it over dinner.

Right now there's something we need to talk about, something really important."

"What have you done?" Mr. Boone asked, suddenly frowning.

"Nothing, Dad. Well, not much anyway. But, look, Ike is on his way over and we need to have a family meeting."

"Ike? A family meeting? Why am I nervous?"

"Can we just meet with Mom in the conference room and talk about it?"

"Sure," Mr. Boone said, putting away his pipe and getting to his feet. He followed Theo downstairs. Ike was knocking on the front door and Theo unlocked it. Mrs. Boone emerged from her office and asked, "What's going on here?"

"We need to talk," Theo said. Mrs. Boone gave Ike a quick hug, the kind you're expected to give but don't really want to. She gave her husband a curious look, like "What's he done now?"

When they were situated around the conference table, Theo told the story: Last Thursday in DC, leaving Ford's Theatre, on the crowded subway, the man who looks like Pete Duffy, the secret video made by Theo, the call to Ike, Ike's quick trip to DC, the second spotting of Duffy, the trailing of Duffy to his run-down apartment building, the FuzziFace software and examination of the photos, and, most importantly, their belief that the man is Pete Duffy.

Mr. and Mrs. Boone were speechless.

Ike had his laptop, and it took Theo only a few seconds to wire it to a big screen on a wall at the end of the conference table. "Here it is," Theo said, and the video began in slow motion. Theo froze it and said, "This is the best shot right here." It was an image of the left side of the man's face just as he dipped his newspaper.

Ike pecked on his keyboard and the screen split between that image and one of Pete Duffy taken from an old newspaper photo. Side by side, the men looked somewhat similar.

Mrs. Boone finally said, "Well, I suppose it sort of looks like the same man."

Mr. Boone, always the skeptic, said, "I'm not so sure."

"Oh, it's him," Ike said with little doubt.

"He even walks like Pete Duffy," Theo added.

"And when did you see Mr. Duffy walk?" his father asked.

"During his trial. We walked behind him and his lawyers during the first day of the trial. I remember it clearly."

"Have you been reading spy novels again?" Mrs. Boone asked. She and Mr. Boone were still staring at the images on the screen. Theo did not answer.

"What do you have in mind?" Mr. Boone asked Ike.

"Well, we have to go to the police, show them the video, show them these images, and tell them everything we know. At that point, it's up to them."

The four pondered this for a moment, then Ike continued, "But that, of course, might present another problem. We have a good police department, but Pete Duffy has a lot of friends. There could be leaks. A stray word here or there, then a quick phone call, and Duffy could disappear into thin air."

"Are you suggesting Duffy might have a mole inside our police department?" Mrs. Boone asked, her eyebrows arched with skepticism.

"It wouldn't surprise me," Ike replied.

"Me neither," added Mr. Boone.

Theo was shocked by the suggestion. If you can't trust the police, who can you trust?

Another long pause as the four stared at the screen and considered the situation. "What are you thinking, Ike?" Mrs. Boone finally asked.

"He's a fugitive, currently number seven on the FBI's Ten Most Wanted list, right? So we go to the FBI and keep it away from the Strattenburg Police."

"Well, whatever we do, we're keeping Theo out of it," Mr. Boone said.

That was perfectly fine with Theo. The deeper he sank into the Duffy matter, the more worried he became. However, it was exciting to think about working with real FBI agents.

"Of course we are," Ike said. "But I suppose they'll want to meet with him and get his version of events. We can keep that all nice and secret."

"And when do you think we should meet with the FBI?" Mr. Boone asked.

"As soon as possible. I'll call them first thing in the morning and arrange a meeting. I'll suggest that we meet right here if that's okay."

"Guess I'll have to miss school tomorrow," Theo said.

"You will not," his mother said sharply. "You were out of class Thursday, Friday, and today. You will not miss tomorrow. If we meet, we'll do it after school. Okay, Ike?"

"Sure."

They invited Ike to dinner at Robilio's, their Monday night place, but he declined saying he needed to get back to the office. Theo was relieved, because Ike at dinner would mean a lot of talk about the Duffy case, and Theo had had enough of it for the moment.

He puttered around the office for half an hour, then left for home with Judge. At seven o'clock sharp, the Boone

family settled around its favorite table in the restaurant and
ordered the same food they had eaten the week before, and
the week before that. As they waited, Theo began a lengthy
review of his trip to Washington. As always, his parents
peppered him with questions—about the museums and
monuments, the hotel, the other kids. Did everyone behave?
Any problems whatsoever? What was his favorite attraction?
And so on. Theo unloaded every detail he could possibly
remember, except perhaps for some of the behavior on the
bus. He held their attention with a thorough description of
Ford's Theatre, along with a play-by-play account of Lincoln's
assassination. At the Vietnam Veterans Memorial, he had
found the name of Joel Furniss, the young soldier Ike had
known as a kid and the county's first casualty. He loved the
Washington Monument, the space museum, and the other
war memorials, but was bored with most of the Smithsonian.

Mrs. Boone asked him if he would like to return to DC
and spend an entire week seeing the other sights. She and
Mr. Boone had talked about going there for their summer
vacation. Theo wasn't so sure. At the moment, he'd seen
enough.

He went to bed early and slept for nine hours.

# Chapter 6

Early Tuesday morning, while Theo was in school, Ike contacted the FBI office in Northchester, an hour away from Strattenburg. The first phone call led to a second, then a third as the matter became urgent. Calls were made to Theo's parents, and a meeting was arranged.

Theo was having lunch with April Finnemore when the principal, Mrs. Gladwell, appeared from nowhere and whispered, "Theo, your mother just called and you're being excused. She wants you to get to her office as soon as possible."

Theo had a pretty good idea what was going on, but he said nothing to April. He got his backpack, checked with Miss Gloria at the front desk, and hopped on his bike.

Minutes later, he wheeled to a stop behind Boone & Boone.

They were waiting for him: his parents, Ike, and two FBI agents. The white one was named Ackerman and was a little older, with some gray in his dark hair, and he greeted Theo with a frown, which would turn out to be permanent. The black one was named Slade, thin as a rail and with a mouthful of perfect teeth. Everyone suffered through a few minutes of nervous chatter before they got down to business. Theo told his story. Ike ran the video, then did the comparison of Duffy images. Back to Theo, who began answering the agents' questions. His parents sat beside him, quiet but ready to protect him if need be. Ackerman asked if they could have a copy of the video. Mrs. Boone said certainly. After half an hour of discussion, Slade stepped out of the conference room to call his boss back at the office.

Elsa brought in some sandwiches and managed to shoot Theo a serious look as if to ask, "What on earth have you done now?" He tried to ignore her. As they ate, the two agents politely asked Theo some of the same questions over and over, taking notes the entire time, pinning down the details. Time of day, Metro stations, number of cars in the train, exact location of "the subject." They did not refer to him as Pete Duffy; he was always "the subject." An hour passed as they watched the video again, talked, and waited on word from the FBI office in Northchester. Mrs. Boone left to make a few phone calls, and when she returned Mr. Boone went upstairs to check on some pressing matters. Once, both agents were on their cell phones, backs turned to the others, almost whispering important details. When one wasn't on the phone, the other one was. As the afternoon dragged on, they became more animated. It seemed, at least to Theo, that they had managed to get the attention of more important FBI people.

Around two p.m., Slade got off his phone, placed it on the table, and said, "Okay, here's the plan right now. We've sent the video and photo to our office in Washington. Our experts are going through it now, but their quick analysis is that there is an eighty percent chance this guy is the real Pete Duffy. We'll have several agents on the Metro this afternoon, and we'll also stake out the apartment on Forty-Fourth Street. There is an outstanding warrant for his arrest, so the paperwork is already in place. If our guys see him, they'll grab him, search him, search his apartment, and, with luck, we'll have our man."

Ackerman said, "We need to get back to our office now, but we'll be in touch."

Slade looked at Theo and said, "On behalf of the FBI,

Theo, we want to say a big thanks for doing what you've done. It took a very sharp eye to see what you saw."

Ackerman turned to Ike and said, "And to you as well, Mr. Boone. Thank you for getting involved."

Ike waved him off as if it was no big deal. Just another day at the office.

After the agents left, Mrs. Boone looked at her watch and said, "Well, I guess it's too late to go back to school."

"Of course it is," Theo said helpfully. "I think I should stick around here and wait to hear from the FBI. They might need me again."

"I doubt that," Mr. Boone said, also glancing at his watch. Time to get to work.

When his parents were gone from the room, Theo smiled at Ike and said, "It must be cool to be an FBI agent, don't you think, Ike?"

Ike grunted his disapproval. "Listen, Theo, about the time you were born I got into some trouble and the FBI came knocking on my door. It was not pleasant. When you're on the other side of those guys, it's hard to be a big fan. They're good, and they know it, but they're not always right."

Ike's troubles were deep, family secrets. Theo, being the nosy kid, had fished around a few times for details from his parents, but had learned nothing. Now that Ike had opened the door, Theo was tempted to go barging in. But he bit his tongue and said nothing.

Ike said, "Just think about it, Theo. Right now your video is being analyzed by the best experts in the world. Pretty cool, right?"

"Very. Say, Ike, we haven't talked about this, but have you thought about the reward money? They're offering a hundred thousand dollars for information leading to the arrest and conviction of Pete Duffy. I'm sure you know this, right?"

"Sure, everybody knows it. And, yes, I've thought about it. What will you do with that kind of money?"

"Well, I think you should get some of it. What if we just split it, okay?"

"We're not there yet, Theo. First, they've got to catch him. Then there's the small matter of another trial. Duffy has great lawyers and he'll put up a strong defense, just like last time. You watched the trial and you know that the prosecution was about to lose when Judge Gantry declared a mistrial. Getting a conviction will not be easy."

"I know. I was there, but that was before we knew about Bobby Escobar. He's an eyewitness, Ike. He saw Pete Duffy sneak into his home at the exact time his wife was killed. And he found the golf gloves Duffy was wearing when he strangled his wife."

"Right. Let's just wait until there's a conviction, and then we'll talk about the reward money."

"Okay. But what would you do with fifty thousand?"

"Theo."

At four thirty, Theo was at his desk in his office, with his dog at his feet, doodling at his homework and staring at a Twins clock on the wall. He closed his eyes and imagined the crowded Metro train as it stopped at the Judiciary Square Station.

A dozen FBI agents in various disguises are on the train, watching, waiting. The doors open, a crowd of commuters rushes into the train. One of them is Pete Duffy, and he is soon identified by an agent who whispers into a mike. "PD is identified, car number four, halfway back." Duffy reads his newspaper, clueless that his life as a fugitive is about to end. Clueless that he is about to be arrested and hauled back to Strattenburg. At the Metro Center Station, even more agents pile on board; some maneuver so close to Duffy they could touch him. But they wait. They're patient, professional. They whisper into their mikes, text messages on their cell phones, ride the train as if they do it every day, and before long they're at the Tenleytown Station. Duffy folds his newspaper, sticks it under his arm, gets to his feet, and when the train stops and the doors fly open, he steps onto the platform, same as everyone else. More agents are waiting at the station. They trail Duffy up through the quiet, leafy streets of Northwest Washington, watching every step. When he turns on 44th Street, he comes face-to-face with armed men in black trench coats. One says, "FBI, Mr. Duffy, you're under arrest." Duffy almost faints, or does he? Is he relieved that his life as a fugitive is over? Probably not. Theo suspects Duffy would prefer to live on the run. They handcuff him and lead him to an unmarked van. He says nothing, not a single word. At the jail he calls his lawyer.

At five o'clock, Theo was staring at the phone on his desk. He called Ike, who'd heard nothing and said to relax. They'll get Duffy, but maybe not today. Maybe not tomorrow. Be patient.

*Really, Ike?* Theo said to himself. *How many thirteen-year-olds understand how to be patient?*

After dark, and without a peep from the FBI, the Boone family walked three blocks from their office to the Highland Street Shelter, where they volunteered each week. They began in the kitchen where they donned aprons and served soup and sandwiches, always with smiles and warm greetings. Most of the faces were well known—they either lived there or showed up week after week. Theo even knew the names of some of the kids. The shelter provided permanent housing to about forty homeless people, including a few families. It also fed a hundred every day at lunch and dinner. After everyone was served, the Boones grabbed a quick bite while standing in a corner of the dining room. Vegetable soup with corn bread and a coconut cookie for dessert. It wasn't Theo's favorite meal, but it wasn't the worst either. Every time he ate at the shelter he watched the faces of the people. Some were blank and distant, as if they weren't sure where they were. Most, though, were just happy to have another warm meal.

Mrs. Boone, along with several other female lawyers in town, had started a free legal clinic at the shelter to help women and their families. After dinner, she went to a small room and began seeing clients. Theo went to a play area where he helped kids with their homework. Mr. Boone set up shop at one of end of a dining table and began reviewing documents for homeless people who'd been evicted from their apartments.

At eight twenty, Theo got a text from Ike. *Call me now.* He stepped outside and punched the number on speed dial.

"Just talked to the FBI," Ike said. "Agent Slade called me with an update. Everything went as planned, said they had about a dozen agents involved, but no sign of Duffy.

Nothing. They watched his apartment for three hours and didn't see him. They didn't search it, can't really do that until they have him in custody."

"So, what does this mean?"

"Not sure, really. Duffy is a smart guy and he could be staying at more than one place. Maybe he saw a suspicious person; somebody stared a bit too long. Who knows?"

"What's the plan?"

"They'll try again tomorrow. They'll watch his apartment all night, see if he comes out in the morning, and they'll monitor the trains. But you know how it is; there are about a million people on the Metro during rush hour. I'll call when I hear something."

Theo was devastated. He was certain the FBI, with its unlimited manpower and technology, would have Pete Duffy in custody by midnight.

He walked into the shelter to tell his parents.

# Chapter 7

On Wednesday, during Madame Monique's first-period Spanish class, Theo's mind kept drifting far away to the streets of Washington. He was consumed with the troubling notion that he had done something bad. What if he, in fact, identified the wrong man? Now, thanks to him, dozens of FBI agents and experts were wasting their time riding trains, following the wrong people, poring over a useless video, and in general—in the words of Ike Boone—"chasing their tails."

During Miss Garman's second-period Geometry class, Theo was struck with the horrible thought that perhaps he might get into some trouble. What if the FBI became angry with him for accusing the wrong man? And what if this man somehow found out that he, Theodore Boone, had secretly caught him on video and called in the FBI? Could he be arrested? Or sued for slander?

At lunch, Theo could hardly eat. April knew something was wrong, but Theo said that his stomach was bothering him. And it was. She fished around for the real story, but Theo clammed up and revealed nothing. How do you tell anyone, even a close friend, that you're involved with the FBI, and that maybe you've made a big mistake? He suffered through Chemistry with Mr. Tubcheck, PE with Mr. Tyler, study hall with Mr. Mount, then asked to be excused from debate practice. He counted the minutes until the final bell, then sprinted to the safety of Boone & Boone. Neither of his parents had heard from the FBI. He called Ike but couldn't get an answer.

As he was hiding in his office, with Judge at his feet, Elsa barged in with a plate of cupcakes she said she had made just for him. She insisted he come sit with her in the reception room and tell her about his trip to Washington. Theo had no choice, though he didn't really like her cupcakes. Judge followed him to the front of the building where he sat for half an hour talking to Elsa as she answered the phone and went about her business of running the firm. At one point, his mother walked through the reception area and asked if he'd finished his homework. Theo said almost. Ten minutes later his father ambled through, holding some papers, saw Theo and asked if he'd finished his homework. Theo said almost. Elsa got rid of a phone call and said, "I guess you'd better finish your homework."

"Looks like it," Theo said, and walked back to his office. Because his parents were lawyers, there were a lot of rules in the family. One of the more irksome ones was that they expected Theo, when he was just hanging around the office in late afternoons, to hit the books and finish his homework. They expected near perfect grades, and Theo usually delivered. There was an occasional B on his report card, but nothing they could really complain about. When he got a B and they raised their eyebrows, he asked if they'd made straight A's when they were kids. Well, of course. Didn't all parents make straight A's back in the glory days? He'd made a C in the fourth grade, in math, and he thought they might put him in Juvenile Detention. One lousy C and the entire world almost came to an end.

He couldn't concentrate and the homework was boring, as always.

Ike called just after six p.m. "Just talked to the FBI," he said. "More bad news. They watched the subway again and saw no sign of our man. Looks like he's disappeared again. Vanished."

"That's hard to believe," Theo said. On the one hand,

he was relieved that Duffy was gone and he, Theo, would not get dragged any deeper into the situation. On the other hand, he felt bad for creating this mess. Again, he asked himself why, exactly, had he stuck his nose into this?

"What do you think happened?" he asked.

"Who knows, but there's a good chance ol' Pete isn't as stupid as they think. He's living on the run, a wanted man, and maybe he's learned to see around corners. The FBI comes barging in like a pack of bloodhounds, and Duffy smells trouble. He notices people looking at him, sees some strange faces, and, since he's spooked anyway, he decides to lay low for a while, to change his movements, take a different train, walk down a different street, wear a different suit. There are two million people in Washington, and he knows how to lose himself in a crowd."

"I guess so."

"They watched his apartment building all night, and he didn't go home. That's a good indication he knows something's up. They'll probably never find him now."

"Too bad."

"Anyway, there's not much else we can do at this point."

"Thanks, Ike." Theo stuck his phone in his pocket and went to tell his parents.

Wednesday night dinner meant take-out Chinese from

the Dragon Lady, one of Theo's favorite meals of the week.
They ate on folding trays in the den and watched *Perry
Mason* reruns, another of Theo's favorites. Halfway through
the first episode his mother said, "Theo, you've barely
touched your food."

Theo quickly crammed in a load of sweet-and-sour
shrimp and said, "No way. It's delicious and I'm starving."

She gave him one of those motherly looks that said,
"Sure, but I know the truth."

"Are you worried, Theo?" his father asked.

"About what?"

"Oh, I don't know. Maybe the FBI and the fact that they
can't find Pete Duffy."

"Hadn't thought about it," he said.

His father smiled as he chewed and shot a knowing
glance at Mrs. Boone. When their eyes returned to the
television, Theo reached down and gave Judge half an egg
roll, his favorite of all foods.

Early Thursday morning, Theo was having a quiet breakfast
alone, with his daily bowl of Cheerios and glass of orange
juice, with Judge at his feet having the same, minus the juice.
His father had left early to have breakfast and gossip with

his usual coffee gang downtown. His mother was in the den sipping a diet soda and reading the morning newspaper. Theo was thinking of nothing in particular, was in fact minding his own business and not looking for trouble or adventure, when the phone rang.

His mother called out, "Please get that, Theo."

"Yes, ma'am," he said as he stood and reached for the phone. "Hello."

A somewhat familiar voice said rather stiffly, "Yes, this is Agent Marcus Slade with the FBI. Could I speak to either Mr. or Mrs. Boone?"

"Uh, sure," Theo said as his throat tightened. This is it, he thought in a flash, they're coming after me! They're mad because I've wasted so much of their time. He covered the phone and yelled, "Mom, it's the FBI."

How many eighth graders at Strattenburg Middle School had to deal with the FBI, he asked himself? When his mother picked up the phone in the den, he was tempted to stay on the line and listen in, but quickly changed his mind. Why ask for more trouble? He hid in the doorway that led to the den, just out of sight, and could hear her voice but not her words. When she hung up, Theo scrambled back to his chair and stuck in a mouthful of Cheerios. Mrs. Boone walked into the kitchen, stared at him as if he'd shot someone, and said, "That was the FBI."

*No kidding, Mom.*

"They want to meet with us this morning at the office. They say it's urgent."

On the one hand, Theo was thrilled to be missing school again, but on the other hand reality hit quickly: The FBI was ticked off and they wanted to chew him out face-to-face. He said, "What do they want?"

"The agent wouldn't say. They're driving over now and we'll meet at nine o'clock."

"We? As in me too?"

"Yes, you're invited."

"Gosh, Mom, I hate to miss school," he said with a straight face. And truthfully, at that moment, he'd rather get on his bike and hustle on to class.

An hour later they were hanging around the conference room, waiting on Ike, who was not a morning person at all. He finally arrived, red-eyed and grumpy, and went straight for the coffee. A few minutes later, Agents Slade and Ackerman walked in and everyone said hello. Mrs. Boone closed the door because Elsa was lurking close by, eager to listen in. Vince, the firm's paralegal and one of Theo's closest allies, was also hanging around, curious. And Dorothy, the real estate secretary, had her radar on high alert because all the warning signs were there: (1) Theo was missing school again, (2) Ike was present, and (3) the two FBI agents were back.

Slade went first and began with, "We'll get right to the point. We've seen no sign of Pete Duffy. We think he's changed his routine. We're also convinced that he's the man in the video, and we have reason to believe he's still in Washington, DC." He paused as if waiting for one of the Boones to ask how they knew this, but all Boones were silent. He continued, "We would like Theo and Ike to return to DC and help us with the search."

Ackerman chimed in immediately, "You two have spotted him before. You know what he looks like because you've seen him before, here in Stattenburg. Theo, you said something in our first meeting about recognizing the way he walks, right?"

Theo wasn't sure how to react. He'd been terrified when they all sat down at the table just seconds earlier, but suddenly he was intrigued by the thought of another trip to DC. And this one at the invitation of the FBI! They hadn't come to arrest him—they wanted to join forces. "Uh, right," Theo managed to say.

"Tell us about this," Slade said.

Theo looked to his left, to his mother, then to his father on the right. He cleared his throat and said, "Well, I read this spy novel one time where this American guy was being followed by some Russian spies, the KGB, I think."

"That's right, the KGB," Slade added.

"And the American knew that every face is different and faces are easy to disguise. But, he also knew that every person walks a different way, too, and it's harder to disguise the way you walk. So he put a small pebble in his shoe and it made him walk funny. He lost the Russians and got away. They killed him later, but it wasn't because he had a rock in shoe."

"And you can identify Pete Duffy by the way he walks?" Ackerman asked.

"I don't know about that, but when I followed him off the train last Thursday, I recognized his walk. Nothing strange about it, it's just the way he walks. I saw him several times during the trial here."

Both parents were frowning at him as if he were telling tall tales. Ike, though, was grinning and thoroughly enjoying his nephew.

Mr. Boone said, "Let me get this straight. You want Theo to go back to DC and watch people walk along the streets?"

Slade replied, "That, and to ride the Metro again and hope we get lucky. Theo and Ike. Look, it's a longshot, but we have nothing to lose."

Ike laughed and said rudely, "I love it. The FBI is the most powerful crime-fighting organization in the world, with the best technology money can buy, and you're relying on a thirteen-year-old kid who thinks he can identify a person by the way he walks."

Ackerman and Slade took deep breaths, ignored Ike, and moved on. Slade said, "We'll fly you there and back, take care of all the expenses. Both of you. We'll be with you and you'll be surrounded by FBI agents. There's no danger."

"It sounds dangerous," Mrs. Boone said.

"Not at all," Ackerman replied. "Duffy's not going to harm anyone. He doesn't want trouble."

"How long will Theo be away?" Mr. Boone asked.

Slade said, "Not long. Today is Thursday. If we hustle we can catch a flight today at noon and be in DC in time to catch rush hour on the subway. We do surveillance today, tonight, tomorrow, and he'll be home Saturday."

Theo managed to keep a straight face and hide his excitement. His mother almost ruined it with, "I think one of us should go too, Woods."

Mr. Boone said, "I agree, but I have two big deals to close Friday."

Mrs. Boone said, "And I have to be in court all day tomorrow."

So typical. His parents played an endless game of each trying to appear busier than the other.

Ike said, "Relax. I'll take care of Theo. It's an easy trip, and I agree that there's no danger."

"But he'll miss two full days of school," she said.

This hung over the table like a wicked deal breaker until Slade said, "Yes, and we're sorry about that. But I'm sure Theo can catch up later. This is pretty important stuff here, Mrs. Boone, and we really need Theo and Ike to help us. What do you say, Theo?"

"Well, I really hate to miss school, but if you insist."

The five adults found this amusing.

# Chapter 8

When Theo, Ike, Slade, and Ackerman landed at Reagan National Airport in Washington, they were met by two more FBI agents, both wearing the same dark suit, the same navy tie, and the same serious frown. Quick introductions were made; they shook Theo's hand firmly and treated him as if he were a full-blown adult. One grabbed his overnight bag and said, "This way." A black SUV was waiting outside the Arrivals gate, at the curb, in a No Parking zone, but the airport police seemed to ignore it. They piled inside, and young Theodore Boone was whisked away as if he were a very important person. He and Ike sat in the far back and listened as the four agents chatted about other people they knew inside the FBI. As they flew past the Iwo Jima statue, Theo gazed into the distance and admired the Washington

Monument. Only six days earlier he'd been at the very top, looking down upon the city with pure amazement. They crossed the Potomac River on the Arlington Memorial Bridge and worked their way through traffic.

During the flight, Theo studied maps of the streets and Metro stops of central and northwest DC. He wanted to know exactly where he was at all times. When they turned onto Constitution Avenue, he glanced to his right at the Lincoln Memorial. They passed the Reflecting Pool, and drove along the National Mall and passed the Washington Monument. They turned left onto 12th Street and headed north as the traffic got heavier. Near the Metro Center, they suddenly wheeled to a stop in front of a Marriott Hotel. Again, they parked in a No Parking zone, but the doormen were quickly waved away.

*I guess the FBI doesn't worry about getting towed,* Theo thought.

Check-in had been taken care of. They rode the elevator to the fifth floor and walked briskly to Room 520. An agent said, "Your room is next door, Theo, and Mr. Boone's is next to yours with a connecting door." He looked at Slade and Ackerman and said, "You guys are across the hall."

The door opened and they walked into a large suite filled with more agents, and not a single one was wearing a dark suit. An older guy with gray hair stepped forward with a big smile and said, "Hello, guys, I'm Daniel Frye and I'm the leader of this team. Welcome to DC." It took some time to shake everyone's hand and listen to everyone's name. There were six of them, plus Frye, and all were dressed differently. One wore a maroon jogging suit with "Mississippi State" across the jersey. One wore jeans and hiking boots and looked as though he'd just come out of the woods. A female agent was dressed like a sailor in navy whites. The other female agent could have passed for a homeless person. A skinny white boy looked about the same age as Theo and was dressed like a student, complete with a backpack and an earring. And the sixth one had hair as long as Ike's and looked about as rough. Frye looked like he'd just played a round of golf.

They were all very friendly and seemed amused to be working with a thirteen-year-old kid. Theo was overwhelmed and struggled to keep from grinning like a goofy idiot. The agents were sitting casually around the room. A sofa was covered with jerseys and caps. Daniel Frye said, "Okay, Theo, first things first. What's your favorite sports team?"

"Uh, the Minnesota Twins."

Frye frowned, as did a few of the others. "That's kind of odd. You're not from Minnesota. Why the Twins?"

"Because nobody else in Strattenburg pulls for the Twins."

"Fair enough. Problem is, we don't have any Twins stuff." Frye sort of waved his hand over their collection on the sofa.

"Got any Yankee stuff?" Ike asked.

Theo shot back, "I don't do Yankees," and got a few laughs.

"Okay," Frye said. "What about the Redskins?"

"I'd rather not," Theo said. More laughs.

"Nationals?"

"Sure, I like the Nationals."

"Great. Now we're getting somewhere. We'll put you in that red Nationals jersey with a matching cap."

"No cap," Theo said.

"Well, excuse me. But we think you should wear a cap of some sort, part of a disguise."

"Okay, sure, but not a Nationals cap. I have one of my own."

"Okay, okay. We'll look at it in a minute. Now, if we can proceed, here's the plan." One wall was covered with a huge map of central DC and above it was a row of enlarged photos, all of Mr. Duffy. Frye stepped to the wall and pointed to a spot labeled MARRIOTT. "We're here. The Metro Center Station is just around the corner. That's where you got on last Thursday, right?"

"Yes, sir."

"And Duffy was already on the train, right?"

"Yes, sir."

"By the way we'll use a code name for him. It's Cowboy."

"I don't like the Cowboys, either," Theo said. More laughs.

"Well, who do you like? What's your favorite football team."

"Green Bay Packers."

"Okay, we'll use Packer. Does that suit everybody?" Frye looked at his team. Everyone shrugged. Who really cared what they called him? Frye continued, "Good. We're making a lot of progress here. At four o'clock you and Mr. Boone will ride the subway up to Union Station and catch the four thirty-eight coming back this way. Theo will be in the third car, Mr. Boone in the fourth. We will have people in all the cars, and there will always be an agent within ten feet of you, Theo. At four thirty you and Mr. Boone will be hanging around the Judiciary Square Station, waiting on the train and watching the crowd." Frye was pointing to the map as he spoke. "You'll get back on the train at that point and ride here to the Metro Center. If you see nothing, you'll ride to the Farragut North Station, switch cars, and ride all the way to the Tenleytown Station. At that point you'll get off and hang around there for half an hour. That's where Packer made his exit last week. We thoroughly covered this route on Tuesday and Wednesday, saw nothing of course, and, frankly, right now we're just praying for a miracle."

"How do we communicate?" Ike asked.

"Oh, we have lots of toys, Mr. Boone."

"Can I go by Ike?"

"Sure. Makes it easier." Frye stepped to a small table that was covered with gadgets. He picked one up. "Looks like your typical smart phone, right?" he said. "But it's really a two-way radio. Plug in the earphones, and you and Theo will look exactly like a couple of guys listening to music while you send e-mails or play games." He moved it a little closer to his face. "And if you need to speak, just get it to within eighteen inches of your mouth, press the green button, and speak softly. It will pick up almost anything. We'll all be on the same frequency and listening in. Any one of us can talk to the others at any time."

He looked at Slade and Ackerman and said, "I assume you guys want to join the fun."

Both nodded yes.

"Okay, we'll give you a couple of briefcases and you'll pretend to be lawyers. There are only about half a million in this city, so you should blend in okay. I'll be at the Metro Center Station. Salter here will be at Woodley Park and Keenum will be at Tenleytown. Questions?"

Theo asked, "And what if we spot Packer?"

"I was getting to that. First, don't stare. Is there any chance he might recognize you?"

Theo looked at Ike and shrugged. "I really doubt it. We've never met, never been too close to each other. I saw him when he was sitting in court, but I'm sure he didn't see me. The courtroom was crowded. And I saw him a couple of times out of the courthouse during the trial, but he would not remember me. I mean, I'm just a kid. What do you think, Ike?"

"I doubt it, too, but let's not take any chances."

Frye asked, "Did he look at you last week when you saw him on the train?"

"I don't think so. We didn't make eye contact."

"Okay, if you spot him, don't stare, and as soon as you can without being noticed, press the green button and tell us. Depending on how close he is to you, we'll ask the questions. When it looks like he's about to get off the train, let us know. When he does, follow him but don't get close. By then we'll have people ready to stop him."

The thought of being close by when the FBI nabbed Pete Duffy made Theo's stomach turn a flip. It would be terribly exciting, and he would be considered a hero, but he really didn't want the attention.

Frye convinced Theo to wear a pair of black-frame

glasses as part of his disguise. They spent another ten minutes haggling over the right cap. No one seemed to like the one he brought—a faded, green John Deere number with an adjustable strap. City kids probably wouldn't wear a cap advertising farm machinery, and Theo finally gave in. He agreed on a gray one with a Georgetown Hoyas logo. They decided not to use his backpack, but instead gave him one that was much lighter, just in case he had to move fast once on the streets. He and Ike ran through the workings of their new radios and earphones, and when everything seemed ready, they left and headed for the Metro Center Station.

They boarded and Theo found a seat in the center of the fourth car. Ike, wearing a sports coat, different glasses, khakis and loafers, sat across from him. The guy with the maroon jogging suit was a few feet away, standing. When the train began to move, Theo plugged in his earphones and scanned the crowd. He pretended to be texting when he heard Frye's voice. "How you doing, Theo?"

Theo raised the phone a few inches, pressed the green button, and softly said, "Everything's cool. No sign of Packer."

"We hear you loud and clear."

Theo, Ike, and the jogger got off at the Tenleytown

Station, waited a few minutes, then caught an inbound train. Minutes later, it stopped at the Judiciary Square Station and they got off. That was where the FBI assumed Pete Duffy boarded the train. Theo walked around, lost in his music and texts, the same as the other kids waiting for the train. No sign of Duffy. At the end of the platform, he saw the sailor. At the other end, he saw the skinny student. More commuters arrived and the platform got crowded. In the throng, he saw Slade, looking very much like a lawyer. The train arrived. No one got off and the commuters rushed on board. Theo got swept up with the crowd and found a spot in the middle of the third car. Ike disappeared into the fourth. The jogger was standing five feet from Theo. As the train bolted forward, Theo casually looked around.

Nothing. No one remotely resembled Pete Duffy.

More commuters packed on board at the Metro Center Station. Nothing. At Farragut North, Theo scrambled to leave the third car and climb onto the fifth car. Nothing. Their next, and final, stop was the Tenleytown Station. Several commuters got off, along with Theo, Ike, the jogger, and the sailor. When he felt comfortable, he pressed the green button and said, "Theo, here, and I just got off the train. I've seen no one."

Ike replied: "This is Ike and I've seen nothing."

As instructed they hung around the station until two more trains stopped. Frye instructed them to reboard the inbound train, return to Judiciary Square, and do it all again. For Theo, the excitement was fading. There were so many people using the subway it seemed almost impossible to see them all.

For two hours, Theo and Ike rode the red line, back and forth, between the Tenleytown and Judiciary Square stations.

If Pete Duffy was still in town, he was either riding in cabs or using another subway line. For the third day in a row, the search for him went nowhere.

In his hotel room, Theo changed out of the red Nationals jersey and took off the Georgetown cap. He called his mother and gave a full report. He was thoroughly bored with the subway but still enjoying the hunt. In his opinion, they were wasting their time.

Early Friday, Theo, Ike, and the entire team descended onto the Metro and rode trains for three hours. Nothing. Frye suspended the search at ten thirty, and Theo and Ike returned to the hotel. They killed some time, had a quiet lunch together in the hotel restaurant, and were talking about doing some sightseeing when Frye popped in and invited them to take a tour of the FBI headquarters. They jumped at the invitation and spent two hours in the J. Edgar Hoover Building on Pennsylvania Avenue. At four p.m., they were back on the subway, looking at strangers and seeing no one of interest.

By seven p.m., Theo was thoroughly bored with everything—the subway, the hordes of people, the constant thoughts of Pete Duffy, and the city itself. He just wanted to go home.

# Chapter 9

Agent Daniel Frye was a nice guy, but he was becoming a drill sergeant. He insisted the team work early Saturday, because, who knows, Pete Duffy just might move around some. He had obviously changed his routine, and since Theo and Ike were in town anyway, why not ride a few more subway trains and hope for a miracle? Their flight didn't leave until noon.

Over an early breakfast, Theo and Ike talked about the obvious: If Pete Duffy had not been back to his apartment in four days, he was gone. Something had spooked him and he'd vanished again. They had been lucky once, but their luck had run out.

They devoured pancakes, then met with the team for a final foray into the underground.

A miracle was not in the works. At ten a.m., Theo, Ike, Slade, and Ackerman left the hotel in yet another black FBI van and went to the airport. They checked in and, after a long walk through a concourse, found their gate. They had over an hour to kill, and Theo was immediately bored. He was also tired of this little adventure. Furthermore, he was irritated because he was missing his weekly round of golf with his father.

During the tour of the Hoover building the day before, he had entertained thoughts of becoming an FBI agent, of traveling the world stalking terrorists and the like. Now, though, he dismissed those thoughts and could not imagine a career that involved sitting on subway trains for hours on end. He told Ike he was going to find a restroom and roam around. Ike, his nose stuck in a newspaper, grunted in response. Slade and Ackerman were both on the phone and watching planes take off and land in the distance. The airport was not busy, and as Theo walked along the concourse he passed a bookstore, a gift shop, two bars where some folks were already drinking too much, a sad little quarantine box where the smokers were caged in, and several restaurants. He used the restroom, and as he stepped back onto the concourse to continue his stroll, he bumped into a man who was in a hurry. The contact was slight, but it was enough to make the man drop his carry-on bag.

"Sorry," the man said as he hurried to pick up his bag. When he bent over, his eyeglasses slipped off.

"Sorry, too," Theo said, embarrassed.

As the man grabbed his glasses, Theo looked at him and moved back a step. Something about him was familiar; in fact, he looked a lot like Pete Duffy, but with blond hair and different glasses. He froze for a second, glared at Theo as if he knew him, then smiled as if all was well. Theo froze, too, but quickly remembered Frye's warning: Don't stare. He returned the smile and walked in the opposite direction. Duffy continued on, in a hurry, and Theo ducked behind a newsstand. As he watched Duffy hoof it down the concourse, he realized he'd seen that walk before. He called Ike. Straight to voice mail. He had numbers for both Slade and Ackerman. He called Slade and began trailing Duffy, who was getting farther away. Twice he glanced over his shoulder, as if he knew someone was back there.

Slade answered after the fourth ring. "Yes, Theo."

"I got Packer," Theo said. "Come quick."

"Where?"

"Down the concourse. He just passed gate number thirty-one. He's in a hurry and I think he's trying to catch a flight."

"Stay on his tail. We'll be right there."

Theo moved along the edge of the concourse, trying to

stay out of sight but having trouble keeping up with Duffy. At gate twenty-seven, though, Duffy slowed down and got in the back of a long line of people boarding. He glanced back again, but Theo was hiding behind an information booth. He waited for what seemed like hours until he saw Slade and Ackerman walking rapidly toward him. Ike was trying to keep up.

Theo waved them over. "He's at gate twenty-seven, waiting to board."

"Are you sure it's him?" Ackerman asked.

"Pretty sure. We made eye contact. I think he thought he'd seen me somewhere before."

"Which guy?" Ackerman asked as they peeked around the booth. A lady at the desk asked, "May I help you?"

Slade said, "FBI, ma'am. We're cool."

Theo said, "He's at the back of the line, brown jacket, khaki pants, black carry-on bag. He's got blond hair now." Ackerman looked at the large screen above them and said, "Gate twenty-seven. Delta nonstop to Miami."

Slade said to Ackerman, "Call Frye. Get the flight delayed or grounded or whatever. Let's stay here, let Packer get on board, and at that point there's no escape."

"Right," Ackerman said, punching numbers on his phone.

Slade said, "I'll go get in line behind him, just to make

sure he doesn't disappear." Slade casually strolled down the concourse, like any other passenger, and got in line for the flight to Miami. There were six people between him and Duffy and the line was moving slowly. Duffy seemed a bit jumpy. He was probably wondering where he'd seen that kid before, and he kept glancing down the concourse. Ackerman was talking to Frye. Ike was crouching behind Theo and breathing heavily. The lady at the desk just stared at them. She was probably thinking *This kid ain't no FBI agent*. But she said nothing.

Ackerman stuck his phone in his pocket and said, "Got it. The flight will be delayed until we do our business. Packer won't make it to Miami. Assuming, of course, it is Packer."

"Is it Duffy?" Ike grunted at Theo.

"I sure hope so," Theo replied, and then almost got sick again with the thought that maybe he had picked the wrong guy. What if all this was one big mistake?

But it was Duffy. Theo had seen his eyes, and he'd seen him walk.

As soon as Duffy handed his ticket to the Delta agent and disappeared through the door to the walkway, Slade walked to the counter, flashed his badge to another Delta agent, and said, "FBI. This flight is being delayed."

Ackerman hurried to the gate, with Theo and Ike right behind him. All passengers were on board and the crew was preparing to push back. Ackerman said, "I'll walk on board and see where he's sitting. That way we'll have a name."

"Good idea," Slade said.

Ackerman explained things to the Delta agent and hustled on to the airplane. Five minutes later he was back at the counter. He said, "Seat fourteen B. Who's the passenger?" The Delta agent pecked the keys, scanned the monitor, and said, "A Mr. Tom Carson. Bought the ticket yesterday at a Delta office on Connecticut Avenue."

"Cash or credit card?"

"Uh, let's see. Cash."

"Cash for a one-way ticket?"

"That's right."

"Okay. We think we need to have a chat with him. There is a warrant for an arrest, but first we need to verify his identity and it might take some time. Have your pilot announce that there is a slight delay. No one will be surprised."

"Sure. Happens all the time."


Twenty minutes later, Daniel Frye arrived in a rush with three other agents, all new ones. He huddled with Slade and Ackerman, and he asked Theo, "Are you sure?"

Theo nodded and said, "About ninety percent."

Frye said, "Okay, here's the plan. Let's get the guy off the plane and talk to him. We'll check his paperwork and see where that goes. If it's the wrong guy, then we'll apologize, send him on his way, and hope he doesn't sue us."

Theo and Ike were sitting with their backs to a wall in the spacious waiting area when Frye and Mr. Tom Carson exited the walkway. Carson was either angry or frightened; obviously, he was not very happy. As they were joined by other agents, he saw Theo across the way and shot him a look of murderous hatred.

They took him to an airport office for questioning.

As Theo and Ike waited, they began to worry about their flight. They couldn't leave until they knew for sure if Carson was Duffy/Packer; nor did they want to leave.

Frye, though, was a veteran, and Duffy was an amateur. After fifteen minutes of interrogation, his story crumbled and he finally admitted who he was. His brand-new papers—Maryland driver's license, Social Security card, passport—were all fake. He had a ticket on United from Miami to São Paulo, Brazil, and he had nine thousand dollars in cash in his pocket. He came within fifteen minutes of getting away.

After Frye informed him he was under arrest, he demanded a lawyer and stopped talking.

Theo and Ike were standing on the concourse near the office when they led Duffy away in handcuffs. As he walked past them, he once again glared at Theo.

Special Agent Daniel Frye walked over, as did Slade, Ackerman, and another agent. Frye put his hand on Theo's shoulder and said, "Nice work, kid."

# Chapter 10

It was raining hard when Theo awoke in his own bed early Sunday morning. He said good morning to Judge, who slept under the bed, or sometimes beside the bed, and occasionally even on the bed, but the dog did not open his eyes. Theo opened his laptop and went straight to the Strattenburg morning newspaper, online edition. The headline screamed across the page: PETE DUFFY ARRESTED AT DC AIRPORT. Theo read the story faster than he had ever read anything. He knew the facts—he was searching for his name. His and Ike's. Nothing.

He took a deep breath, and read it again. Acting on an anonymous tip, a team of FBI agents had cornered Duffy after he had boarded a flight to Miami, and so on.

He was bound for São Paulo, Brazil, with fake paperwork and a pocketful of cash. According to an unnamed source, the FBI picked up his trail last week. It was believed that he had been living in the Cleveland Park area for a few weeks. The company that provided the false identity for a Mr. Tom Carson was also under investigation. Duffy was being held in jail in Arlington, Virginia, and was expected to be returned to Strattenburg in the near future. Phone calls to his attorney, Clifford Nance, went unanswered. The local police and prosecutors had no comment.

The story then went on to describe the murder charges against Duffy, details that virtually everyone in town had known for over a year. There was a photo of Myra Duffy, the victim, who had been found strangled in the living room of her home one Thursday morning while her husband, Pete, was playing golf on the course where they lived, at Waverly Creek. There was a photo of Mr. Duffy as he was walking into the courthouse during his trial, a trial that ended when Judge Henry Gantry abruptly stopped things and sent the jury home for good. It was rumored at the time that a mysterious witness had come forward late in the trial, a witness who could place Mr. Duffy inside his home at the time of the murder. This witness has never been identified. Just as his second trial was starting, Duffy disappeared.

Theo knew all this; he'd been in the middle of it.

Now, he was in the middle of it again, and this made him nervous. No, it scared the daylights out of him. Duffy had some dangerous friends. The FBI, though, had assured him and Ike that they would be left out of the official version of the story. So far so good, but Ike didn't trust the local police to keep secrets.

The story went on to say that Duffy not only faced another trial for murder, but an escape charge as well. That carried a maximum sentence of ten years. Theo asked himself how in the world could Duffy wiggle around the fact that he skipped town.

He woke up Judge and went downstairs. His parents were at the kitchen table, still in their pajamas, reading the same newspaper and sipping drinks, black coffee for his father, a diet soda for his mother. After a few sleepy good mornings, Mrs. Boone asked, "Have you seen the newspaper?"

"Yes, I just read it. Didn't see my name."

Both parents forced smiles and nodded. They, too, were worried sick about Theo's involvement. What was he supposed to do? He saw Duffy on the train. The man was wanted for murder. Wouldn't any good citizen do what Theo did?

Yes, they agreed that he had done the right thing, but it sure didn't feel like it. He almost wished he had done nothing.

Theo said, "Looks like he's facing at least ten years in the pen, right?"

Mr. Boone grunted and said, "Sure looks that way. I don't see how he can claim he's not guilty of running away."

Mrs. Boone said, "He'll be lucky if he doesn't get the death penalty."

Theo fixed two bowls of Cheerios, one for him, one for Judge. His parents were lost in the newspaper and seemed worried. "Are we going to church?" Theo asked after a bite.

Mrs. Boone said, "It's Sunday morning, Theo. Why wouldn't we go to church?"

"Just asking, that's all."

*Fine, let's play the quiet game.*

After church and lunch, Theo wanted to get out of the house. He told his mother he was going for a bike ride, with Judge on a leash. She told him to be home before dark. He took off, flying along the shaded streets of his quiet neighborhood. He waved at Mr. Nunnery, an old guy who never left his porch, and he called "Hello" to Mrs. Goodloe, another neighbor but one who couldn't hear.

Once again, Theo was thankful that he lived in a town where kids could ride their bikes anywhere they wanted, with no worries about heavy traffic and a million people on the sidewalks. He could never live in a place like Washington. It was a cool city, a nice place to visit, but Theo needed space. With Judge galloping beside him like the happiest dog in the world, he zigzagged here and there, avoiding downtown where a bored policeman might yell at him for running stop signs. Theo knew many of the policemen in town and they were generally nice guys, but there were a few who felt as though kids on bikes should follow all the rules of the road. One of his favorite places was the campus of Stratten College, where students were always tossing Frisbees and killing time on the wide, green lawns. He liked the college but wasn't sure he would go there. It was very close to home and, at the age of thirteen, he was already thinking about getting away.

The Delmont neighborhood was near the school and a lot of students lived there, in older duplexes and apartment buildings and run-down houses. There were coffee shops, bars, used bookstores—a more rustic version of downtown. He found the street he was looking for, then the small house where Julio Pena and his family had been living for a few months.

The Penas had once lived in the homeless shelter on Highland Street. Theo had met Julio there and had helped him with his homework. He was a seventh grader at Strattenburg Middle School, and Theo saw him occasionally on the playground. His cousin, Bobby Escobar, was the prosecution's star witness against Pete Duffy.

On the day Myra Duffy was murdered, Bobby was working at the Waverly Creek golf course. He had been there for about three months. He had been in the country for about a year, after he entered illegally from El Salvador. Some would call him an "illegal immigrant." Others, an "undocumented worker."

Theo had read in the newspaper that there were about eleven million people like Bobby working and hiding in the country.

At any rate, Bobby was having a quiet lunch under some trees when he saw Pete Duffy suddenly appear in his golf cart, hustle into his home, stay about ten minutes, then hop back into his golf cart and speed away. It was eleven forty-five a.m., the approximate time Myra Duffy was strangled to death. Bobby was afraid to come forward for the obvious reason—he did not want to be deported—but Theo had convinced him to talk to Judge Gantry. This was after the trial had started, and it was the reason the judge declared a mistrial. Since then, the police had promised to protect Bobby and make sure he didn't get into any immigration problems. Mr. and Mrs. Boone were attempting to sponsor him and help him get his citizenship, but that process was moving slowly.

Theo knocked on the door but no one answered. He peeked into the backyard, then hopped on his bike and continued down the street. Some boys were playing a pickup game of soccer in a small park and a lot of people were watching and milling about. Almost all appeared to be Hispanic. Julio was with a group of kids, including his twin siblings, Hector and Rita, behind a goal, kicking a soccer ball and killing time. Theo inched closer until Julio saw him. He smiled, walked over, and said, "Theo, what are you doing here?"

"Nothing really, just out riding my bike."

When the Pena family lived at the shelter, Theo had taught English to Hector and Rita, and when the two kids saw him talking to their brother they ran over to say hello. Judge soon got their attention, and they took the leash and went for a walk. A lot of kids noticed Judge and wanted to pat him on the head and say things to him. It was a proud moment for the dog.

Theo and Julio chatted about this and that, and when the time was right Theo asked, "Say, Julio, how's Bobby doing? Is he still living with you guys?"

Julio frowned and glanced at the soccer game not far away. "He stays with us some, and then he'll go back to his old place. He's still pretty scared, you know? Plus, Bobby and my mother don't always get along."

"That's too bad."

"Yeah, they fight a lot. Bobby likes to drink beer and he brings it home, and this upsets my mother. She doesn't want that stuff in the house, says it's her house, and he has to live by the rules. And I think he might be doing some other bad stuff, you know?"

"I know," Theo said, though he really didn't. "Doesn't sound too good. Is he still working at the golf course?"

Julio nodded.

"Look, Julio, there's something Bobby needs to know. They just found Pete Duffy and arrested him. He's coming back to town for another trial."

"The guy who killed his wife?"

"Yep, and Bobby is about to be a very important person. Has he talked to the police lately?"

"I don't know. I don't see him every day."

"Well, I think you need to talk to Bobby just so he'll know. I'm sure the police will be around shortly to have a chat." Theo wanted to say something about Omar Cheepe and Paco and the other tough guys who were still around, and probably still worked for Pete Duffy, but he didn't want to frighten anyone. If Bobby got scared, he would vanish into the night.

Julio said, "He's thinking about going home. His mother is dying and he's very homesick."

"Your mother's sister?"

"Yes."

"I'm so sorry. But my parents are trying to help him get a work permit. He really shouldn't leave anytime soon, Julio. Can you tell him this?"

"It's his mother, Theo. If your mother were dying wouldn't you want to go home?"

"Sure."

"Plus, he's still pretty nervous about getting involved. Just last week some of his friends who worked in an apple orchard not far from here got arrested because they didn't have the papers, you know, and now they're in jail somewhere, waiting to be sent back to El Salvador. It's not easy living like this, Theo. It may be hard for you to understand, but Bobby doesn't want to be involved. He doesn't trust everyone like you do."

"Okay. I get it."

Hector and Rita were back with Judge, bored with him now and ready to hand over the leash. Judge was tired of the attention and wanted to leave. Theo said good-bye to the Penas and pedaled away.

# Chapter 11

Theo's favorite teacher was Mr. Mount, his homeroom teacher and faculty adviser for the Debate Team. He was in his mid-thirties, still single, and prone to flirting with the young female teachers, and he had a happy, laid-back attitude about life that the boys adored. His family was full of lawyers and he himself had finished law school and worked for one less than pleasant year with a big firm in Chicago. He loved teaching, enjoyed being around kids, and had decided that he belonged in a classroom and not a courtroom. He taught Government at third period, and was often inclined to let the boys discuss whatever they wanted as long as it was remotely related to politics, history, or the law. Also, he gave easy tests.

With Duffy all over the news, there was little doubt

about what the class would dwell on Monday morning.

"I have a question," Darren said not long after Mr. Mount called the class to order.

"What is it, Darren?"

"The newspaper said that Pete Duffy might fight extradition back to Strattenburg. What does that mean?"

Mr. Mount glanced at Theo, but chose to handle it himself. Theo knew more about the law than anyone in the room, except Mr. Mount, but Theo was often reluctant to dominate the discussions. He didn't want to appear to be a know-it-all.

Mr. Mount said, "Good question. Extradition is a legal process whereby a person who is arrested in one state is sent back to the state where the crime occurred. Obviously, this person does not want to return to the place where he's in trouble, so he often tries to block the transfer. It's always a waste of time because eventually the courts see to it that he gets shipped back. The only time it gets sticky is where one state has the death penalty and the other state does not. But even then, the defendant loses. It's more of a problem between countries because the United States does not have extradition treaties with all other countries. You guys ever see the movie *The Great Train Robbery*?"

A few hands went up.

"It's the true story of a train robbery in England, around nineteen sixty or so. This gang stopped a train loaded with money and made a clean escape. Eventually they all got caught, with the exception of one guy who made it down to Brazil, the same place Duffy was headed. At the time, Brazil did not have an extradition treaty with the United Kingdom, and so this guy was able to live a pretty good life down there and the British police couldn't touch him."

"What happened to him?" Darren asked.

"He eventually got homesick and returned to London. I think he died in prison."

"I have another question," Woody said. "My dad says it's unheard of for a guy charged with murder to be able to post a bond and stay out of jail while he's waiting on his trial. Somehow Pete Duffy got around this, and look what happened. He was rich, so he got a special deal, right? My dad says anyone else would've been locked up and not able to run away. I don't understand this bond thing."

Mr. Mount looked at Theo again. Theo said, "Well, your dad is right. Most judges will not even consider a bond in a murder case. For other cases, say for example embezzlement, say you got caught stealing money from your boss, a serious crime but nothing violent, then, your lawyer would ask the judge to set a reasonable bond. The prosecutor always wants a high bond, the defendant a low one. Say the judge sets the bond at fifty thousand dollars. You would then go to a bail bondsman and put up ten percent in cash. He writes the bond, you get out while you wait for your trial, and everybody's happy. If you don't show up in court, the bail bondsman has the right to track you down and bring you back."

"What's the difference between bail and bond?" Woody asked.

"Nothing really. Lawyers use either word. They say 'My client's bond is five thousand dollars,' and they say, 'My client's bail is five thousand dollars.' They mean the same thing."

"So how did Duffy get a bond?"

"He had money. His bail was set at a million dollars, and he put up some land worth that much. He didn't go through a bail bondsman, but his lawyer arranged the deal with the court."

"What happened when he disappeared?"

"The county took his land. Just like that."

"Does he get it back now that he's been found?"

"No. He lost it forever. According to my dad, the county plans to sell the land and keep the cash."

"Can he get another bond now?"

"No, not after jumping bond the first time. No judge would consider bail for an escapee."

"Can we watch the trial again, Mr. Mount?" asked Ricardo.

Mr. Mount smiled and said, "We will try, that's all I can promise. I doubt if it will happen anytime soon."

"I wonder how they caught him," Brian said.

*If you only knew,* Theo said to himself.

During afternoon study hall, Theo asked Mr. Mount if he could be excused for a few minutes. He needed to run some vague errand. Mr. Mount looked at him suspiciously but agreed anyway. Theo might flirt with trouble from time to time, but he would never do anything terrible.

He found Julio on the playground, again playing soccer. Julio took a break from the game and stood next to Theo as they watched the action. "Any luck with Bobby?" Theo asked quietly.

"Yes, I saw him last night. I told him what you told me and he's really nervous. He is wondering why he should get involved in a murder trial. He has everything to lose and nothing to gain, and he really doesn't care if this Duffy guy goes to jail or not. That, plus he's really worried about his mother."

"Can't blame him for that."

"You know, Theo, it would have been better if Duffy was never caught."

"Maybe you're right," Theo said, as he suddenly felt guilty again. But guilty of what? He had spotted a fugitive and done what was right. "Tell Bobby things will be okay, all right, Julio? He's got to cooperate with the police."

"Maybe I'll let you tell him."

"I'll do that."

As he walked back to homeroom, he mentally kicked himself for getting in so deep. He'd stuck his nose into somebody else's business and now he wished he hadn't. The Duffy circus would once again take over the town, and with it there would be the possibility of bad guys poking around. If it somehow leaked that Theo and Ike were responsible for Duffy's capture, things might get rough. And Bobby Escobar might vanish at any moment.

After school, Theo checked in at the Boone & Boone law office. Elsa informed him that he had worn the same shirt twice last week and she was tired of looking at it. He said thanks and went to his office, a small room in the back that was once used for storage. When everyone was busy, he left Judge behind, sneaked out the back door, and rode his bike downtown where he met April Finnemore at Guff's Frozen Yogurt on Main Street.

Theo ordered his favorite—chocolate smothered with crushed Oreos. April never had the same thing twice. She was an artist, a creative type, and always trying something new. Theo didn't understand this, and she didn't understand why Theo was so rigid in his routines. He lived by the clock and rarely tried anything new. He blamed his parents. After sampling three types, while Theo waited impatiently, she finally selected pistachio with walnuts.

Walnuts? But Theo said nothing. They found their favorite booth, one with privacy. She began firmly with, "Now, I want to know why you missed school last Thursday and Friday."

"I'm not supposed to say."

"You've been acting weird, Theo. What's going on?"

April was the one friend who could keep secrets. She came from a broken family where there was a lot of strange behavior, a lot of goofiness that would be embarrassing if people knew about it. Thus, she had learned to stay quiet at an early age. She could also spot trouble. If Theo was worried or frightened or in a foul mood, leave it to April to zero in with her usual, "Okay, Theo, what's going on?" He always told her and he always felt better. She told him things, too, usually stuff about her family, but also her dreams of getting away, of becoming a great artist and living in Paris. Most boys would have little patience with such foolishness, but Theo adored April and he was always willing to listen.

He took a bite, wiped some Oreos off his lip with a

napkin, looked around to make sure no one was listening, and said, "Well, have you seen this story about Pete Duffy getting caught?"

"Of course. It's all over the news."

"Here's what really happened."

He told her everything.

"But, Theo, what you did was brave and honorable. You're responsible for bringing a murderer to justice. At the moment when you saw him and realized who he was, you had no choice but to do what you did. I'm very proud of you. I can't think of another kid who could have done that. You caught him twice."

"But what if he knows who I am? If you had seen the look on his face when they walked him away in handcuffs, you'd be pretty scared."

"He's not going to hurt you. He's in enough trouble. Besides, I doubt if he recognized you. You've never met the man. You're just a thirteen-year-old kid he saw in the airport when he must have been in shock. I wouldn't worry about that."

"Okay, what about Bobby Escobar? He's about to be on the hot seat and he's probably terrified. I've really complicated his life."

"He's also the star witness. You gotta believe the police will take care of their star witness. Right?"

"I guess. But Duffy has some thugs I sort of bumped into during the first trial. They're probably still around."

"Maybe not. They might've skipped town when Duffy did. And let's say they are still here. What do they gain by harming you? You're just a kid. If they beat you up, how does that help Duffy with his murder trial?"

"I won't care if I'm beat up."

"Relax, Theo, you're worrying too much."

"Okay, here's something else to worry about. This is a long shot, but I do think about it. Let's say Duffy goes to trial, gets convicted of murder, and the jury gives him the death penalty. Then one day they walk him into the death chamber down at Deep Rock Prison, put a needle in his arm, and it's lights-out. If they execute him, I'll get some of the blame."

"Look, Theo, you always say you believe in the law, right?"

"Of course."

"And the law in this state says that if a person is convicted of capital murder, then that person deserves the death penalty. I don't agree with that, but it's the law. Nobody will blame you just because they followed the law."

Theo swallowed some frozen yogurt and tried to think of something else to worry about. Thinking of nothing, he said, "You don't believe in the death penalty?"

"No, I think it's awful. Don't tell me you want the state to execute people."

"I don't know, to be honest. My dad is in favor of capital punishment. My mom agrees with you. They argue about it and I hear both sides. What are you supposed to do with serial killers and terrorists?"

"That's why we have prisons, to lock up nasty people and keep them away from us."

"So, if they prove Pete Duffy strangled his wife just to collect a million bucks in life insurance, you think he should be sent to prison for the rest of his life?"

"Yes. What do you think they should do with him?"

"I don't know. I'll have to think about it. But if his thugs come after me, then I'm in favor of the death penalty."

"Relax, Theo. You're worrying too much."

"Thanks, April. I always feel better when I talk to you."

"That's what friends are for, Theo."

"And please don't tell anyone."

"Stop worrying."

Ike wasn't worried either. He was sipping on a beer and listening to old Motown tunes when Theo and Judge arrived for the mandatory Monday afternoon meeting.

"Any news?" Theo asked. Ike drank and played poker

with some old guys, retired judges and policemen, even some shadier types who had never been caught by the police and had never faced judges. He took great pride in collecting the gossip.

"There's a rumor that Duffy will not fight extradition. He could be back here in a couple of days. Things are looking bad for the old boy. He's broke and probably can't afford to hire Clifford Nance again, probably can't hire any lawyer with any talent. He lost a million bucks on his bond, and that lovely home out in Waverly Creek is about to be owned by the bank."

"Who'll be his lawyer?"

"I have no idea. He'll find someone, some hungry lawyer looking for a big case. Would you take his case, Theo, if you were a young lawyer in town? You say you want to be a big courtroom lawyer."

"I don't think so. He looks pretty guilty."

"He's innocent until proven guilty. Lawyers don't always get to choose their clients, and most criminal defendants are guilty anyway. Someone has to represent him."

"He's guilty of escape. That's ten years right there. Not much a lawyer can do with that."

"Right. I have a hunch Duffy might want to cut a deal, a plea bargain. He pleads guilty to the murder, avoids a trial, and in return the state agrees not to pursue the death penalty. Happens all the time. He'll spend the rest of his life in prison, where he belongs, but at least he'll be alive."

"How bad is prison, Ike?" Theo asked cautiously. It was a subject that had always been off-limits.

Ike kicked back and put his feet on his desk. He sipped beer from the bottle and thought for a long time. "You could say I got lucky, Theo, because I was not in a terrible prison. They're all bad, you know, because you're locked away and forgotten. I lost everything, including my family. My name, respect, profession, self-worth, everything. That's what you think about when you're in prison—all the things you take for granted. It was awful, just awful. But, I was not in a place where bad things happened to us. Sure there was some violence, but I never got hurt. I made friends. I met other men who had been there much longer, and they were surviving. We had jobs, got paid, read thousands of books, had access to newspapers and magazines, watched television, sometimes old movies, wrote letters, exercised. The food was terrible but I actually got healthier in prison because I stopped smoking and drinking and jogged every day." He took another sip and stared at a wall. "The prison Duffy will go to will be much worse, but it will still be something he can survive. If he goes to death row and waits for an execution, he'll be placed in a cell by himself and locked up there for twenty-three hours a day. Bottom line, Theo, if I were Pete Duffy, I'd beg for a plea bargain and avoid death row. He'll be alive and that's worth a lot."

"Will the state offer him a plea bargain?"

"Don't know and it's too early to speculate. Jack Hogan is a very good prosecutor and it'll be his decision."

"I really want to watch another trial."

"Sorry, but you don't get a vote."

The phone on Ike's desk rang and he glanced at the caller ID. "I need to take this."

# Chapter 12

Two days later the big news spread through Strattenburg. Pete Duffy would not fight extradition and was on his way back to town. On the late news Wednesday night, the lead story was the arrival of Mr. Duffy, and a television crew filmed him from a distance as he got out of the backseat of an unmarked car and shuffled through a side door of the jail. He was handcuffed and his ankles were obviously chained together. He wore a cap and sunglasses, and he was surrounded by policemen. It was just a brief glimpse of him, but enough to get Theo excited.

He was watching the news with his parents. It was past his bedtime, but they were ignoring the clock so he could see this breaking story. The reporter said that, according to an unnamed source, Mr. Duffy would make his first appearance in court on Friday.

Theo began scheming of ways to skip school and be in the courtroom.

"How does this make you feel, Theo?" his mother asked.

Theo shrugged and wasn't sure how he felt.

She said, "If not for you, Duffy would be in South America right now. A free man, and probably free for the rest of his life."

On the one hand, Theo sort of wished Duffy was down there, but on the other, he was excited to see him back in town and staring at another trial. Theo said, "I know we're supposed to presume he's innocent until proven guilty, but that's kind of hard to do right now. If he were innocent, why did he run away like he did?"

Mrs. Boone said, "It's difficult because he is guilty of escape and evasion. That's pretty clear."

"Ike thinks he'll try to get a plea bargain," Theo said.

"I doubt that," said Mr. Boone, always quick to disagree with Ike. "Why would he agree to accept a life sentence with no chance of ever getting out?"

"To save his neck," Mrs. Boone said, always quick to disagree with her husband, at least on legal matters. "He's facing the death penalty, Woods."

"I know that."

The reporter walked a few steps and said hello to Jack Hogan, the longtime prosecutor for Stratten County. She asked Mr. Hogan about the details of Duffy's capture in DC, but Hogan said he could not discuss the matter.

For a second, Theo couldn't breathe.

Then she asked Hogan about the charges Duffy was facing. Same as last time, he replied. Murder, first of all. And now, obviously, escape. When would Duffy make his first court appearance? That had not yet been determined, Hogan replied, and it was clear he wasn't saying much. The reporter finally thanked him and signed off.

"Bedtime," Mrs. Boone said, and Theo trudged up the stairs with his dog at his heels.

Judge had no trouble falling asleep under the bed, but Theo couldn't keep his eyes closed. At some point in the long, dark night, a brilliant idea came to him. Mr. Mount required a ten-page research paper to be turned in at the end of the semester. Theo would write his about the preliminary matters that take place before a big criminal trial. There were all sorts of important maneuvers in the early stages as the lawyers tried to gain advantage. They argued about bail. They filed motions to change venue, or move the trial to another city. They fought hard over what evidence should or should not be presented to the jury. And so on. Most people were not aware of all the work that went into a trial long before it ever started.

Theo, though, would explain it all in his research paper. And, if Mr. Mount agreed, Theo would need to spend a lot of time in court.

The more he thought about it, the more he realized how brilliant it was.

Mr. Mount liked the idea, too. Theo was so excited it was impossible to say no. That was Thursday. On Friday, Theo informed him that he needed to be in court at one fifteen for Pete Duffy's first appearance since being hauled back to Strattenburg. To be in court on time meant Theo had to be excused from PE class by Mr. Tyler, and study hall by Mr. Mount himself. Theo had to haggle with Mr. Tyler for a few minutes before he gave in. It was, after all, Friday afternoon, and Theo was normally exempt from PE anyway. He had an asthma problem that he used to his advantage whenever necessary.

So, at ten minutes after one, Theo and Ike were sitting in a courtroom that was buzzing with excitement since quite a few other curious folks showed up for a look at Mr. Duffy. Theo recognized most of the clerks and bailiffs. There was the usual collection of bored lawyers who hung around the courtroom, doing little but trying to look important. There were at least three reporters and a few off-duty policemen. At the defendant's table, Mr. Clifford Nance was chatting with two other lawyers. At the prosecution's table, Mr. Jack Hogan and his crew were reading some documents that must have been difficult to read, judging by their frowns.

A door opened and two large deputies stepped into the courtroom. Behind them was Pete Duffy, in an orange city jail jumpsuit, his wrists and ankles cuffed and chained. Everyone stopped talking and stared in disbelief. It was really him. Caught! The rich guy with the expensive suits and confident air was now reduced to the status of a lowly inmate in the city jail. The handsome, well-groomed gentleman now looked like a lowlife with badly dyed blond hair and an unshaven face.

The deputies quickly unshackled him. He rubbed his wrists as they led him to a chair at the defendant's table. Clifford Nance leaned down and said something to him. Duffy looked wildly around the courtroom, startled at the number of people there to observe him. He looked frightened and disoriented, like he couldn't believe he was back.

In the front row behind the bar, where the spectators sat, Theo caught a glimpse of Omar Cheepe, one of Duffy's men.

A bailiff called court to order, everyone stood, and Judge Henry Gantry appeared from a door in the rear. He tapped his gavel and asked everyone to have a seat. Not wasting time, he looked at the defendant and said, "Would you approach the bench?"

Duffy stood and took a few steps to a spot in front of the bench. He looked up. Judge Gantry looked down. Clifford Nance slowly made his way over to stand beside his client.

"You are Pete Duffy?" the judge asked.

"I am."

"Welcome home."

"Thank you."

"Is Mr. Clifford Nance here still your lawyer?"

"He is."

"You are still charged with the capital murder of your wife, Ms. Myra Duffy. Do you understand this?"

"I do."

"Do you wish to plead guilty or not guilty?"

"Not guilty, Your Honor."

"And you are also charged with escape. Have you discussed this charge with your attorney?"

"Yes, Your Honor."

"And how do you wish to plead?"

"Not guilty."

"Thank you. You may be seated."

Duffy and Nance sat down. Judge Gantry said he wanted the case to proceed as rapidly as possible, would not tolerate delays by either side, and was quite eager to set a trial date. Clifford Nance mentioned the possibility of a hearing on the issue of bail, and Judge Gantry cut him off. No, Mr. Duffy would be spending his days and nights in jail as he awaited trial. Bail was not a possibility. Nance seemed to know this was coming. Everyone else did too. The lawyers went back and forth arguing about how much time they needed to prepare.

Theo whispered to Ike, "I thought you said Duffy wouldn't be able to afford Nance this time around."

Ike whispered, "Anything is possible. Everyone thinks Duffy is broke. Maybe he's got some loot stashed away. Maybe Nance will work cheaper just so he can stay involved. Who knows?"

Ike often spouted off screwball theories with nothing to back them up. Theo suspected he spent too much time gossiping with his old retired buddies, all of whom were over the hill and prone to speculate about things without having any facts.

Theo was being careful. He was sitting low and ducking behind the person in front of him. He did not want to make eye contact with Pete Duffy. Sure the guy was in jail and should probably be considered harmless, but Theo wanted to keep his distance. They had looked each other in the eyes last Saturday at the airport in DC, and Duffy might remember. Of course, Theo was partially disguised then. He had discussed this with Ike, but Ike didn't frighten too easily.

Then there was Omar Cheepe, a shady-looking character known to hang around Clifford Nance's office and do his dirty work. He had a sidekick named Paco; just a couple of thugs.

When the hearing was over, Theo had two choices. He could hop on his bike and hustle back to school, or he could suggest having a frozen yogurt with Ike at Guff's just down the street. He knew Ike would never say no, and that his uncle would happily buy the treat.

Theo ordered the usual—chocolate drenched with crushed Oreos. Ike had a small serving of mango with black coffee. "I have a question for you, Ike," Theo said, then shoveled in an impressive spoonful of frozen yogurt.

"I'm sure you do," Ike said. "You always have questions."

"As I understand the way things work, before the trial, both sides will be required to give the other a list of their witnesses. Right?"

"Right. It's called discovery. Not only the names of the witnesses, but brief summaries of what their testimony will be."

"So the identity of Bobby Escobar will be known to Duffy and his lawyers. They will find out that the prosecution has a witness who'll say he saw Duffy dash into his home at the same time his wife was strangled. Right?"

"Normally, yes."

"Normally? Is there an exception to the rule?"

"I think so. As I recall from my days in the trenches, the prosecution can ask the judge to allow it to withhold the name of a witness if that witness needs to be protected. It's the result of some of the old Mob cases where the star witness against a Mafia leader was a snitch from within the organization. If his identity had been revealed, they would have found the guy at the bottom of a lake wearing concrete boots."

"That makes sense."

"I'm glad you approve. In this case, I'll bet Jack Hogan and the police will try their best to keep Bobby's identity a secret until the last possible moment."

"I sure hope so. I saw that creep Omar Cheepe in the courtroom. I'm sure Paco is lurking somewhere in the shadows. If they find out about Bobby, it could be dangerous."

"I wouldn't worry too much, Theo. Hogan knows he doesn't have much of a case without Bobby. You remember the first trial. It was going badly for the prosecution and

Duffy was about to walk free. Hogan and the police will protect the boy."

"You think I should warn him?"

"No, I think you've done enough. It's a dangerous situation and you need to keep your nose out of it. Okay?"

"I guess."

Ike reached over and grabbed a wrist. With a hard frown, he said, "Listen to me, Theo. Butt out, okay? It's none of your business."

"Well, it sort of is. Bobby Escobar wouldn't be involved if I hadn't convinced his cousin Julio that he should come forward. And, we wouldn't be having this conversation if I hadn't spotted Duffy on the subway."

"True. Nice work. Now leave it alone. You can write your research paper. We'll watch the trial and hope justice prevails. Just stay on the sidelines, okay?" Ike released his wrist.

"Okay," Theo said reluctantly.

"Now, you need to get back to school."

"I don't think so, Ike. It's Friday afternoon and I've had a tough week."

"A tough week. You sound like a workingman who puts in forty hard hours in a factory."

"Look, Ike, even kid lawyers have tough weeks."

# Chapter 13

Across Main Street and four blocks east of Guff's Frozen Yogurt, another meeting was underway and the topic was also the Duffy trial. Clifford Nance had a splendid office on the second floor of what had once been the finest hotel in town; in fact, Mr. Nance owned the entire building and used most of it to house his busy law firm. From his high, arching windows he had great view of the streets below, the courthouse, even the river in the distance. Not that he had much time to enjoy the view; he did not. He was an important lawyer and one of the most prosperous in town.

He was at his desk sipping coffee and chatting with a young lawyer named Breeland, one of the many associates who took orders from him. Nance was saying, "When Judge

Gantry stopped the first trial and sent everybody home, he explained to me and Jack Hogan the following morning that a surprise witness had come forward and had information that was crucial to finding the truth. He would not tell us the name of this witness, nor would he tell us what the witness might say. He left us completely in the dark. We were preparing for the retrial, and at some point Jack Hogan would have been required to disclose the names of all of his witnesses. Before this happened, of course, our dear client skipped town."

"So we still have no clue about this witness?" Breeland asked.

"None whatsoever. Now, though, I suppose we'll find out soon enough."

"And what do we do?"

"Depends on who he is and what he'll say."

"Sounds like a job for Omar."

"Not yet. But remind me to remind him that threatening a witness for the prosecution is a serious crime."

"Omar knows that."

Breeland's cell phone vibrated. He glanced at it and said, "Well, speaking of the devil. Omar is downstairs and wants to talk."

"Send him up."

Omar entered the office and took a seat next to Breeland. Nance said rudely, "I have a meeting in ten minutes, so talk fast."

"Okay," Omar said. "I was just at the jail talking to Duffy. That little Boone kid was in the courtroom this afternoon—don't know how he manages to skip so much school—but he was there with his crazy uncle. I saw them. Pete saw them, and Pete swears he saw them last Saturday at the airport in DC when the Feds snatched him. He can't figure that one out. But if you'll remember, the night before Judge Gantry declared a mistrial, we saw him walk to the Boone & Boone law firm and meet with the family, including the kid and the crazy uncle. Next day—Bam! A mistrial. Something strange is going on here."

"But the Boones are not criminal lawyers," Mr. Nance said. "I know them pretty well."

"Maybe it's not them. Maybe it's just the kid," Omar said. "The kid has his nose stuck in the middle of Pete's case, and his parents are just trying to protect him."

"You can't follow a kid around town, Omar," Breeland said.

"The kid knows who the mysterious witness is," Omar said. "I'll bet good money on it."

Nance and Breeland studied each other for a moment.

Omar continued, "And, I'll bet the kid had something to do with the Feds finding Pete. They were in DC the week before he got nailed."

"Who?" Nance asked.

"The entire eighth grade at Strattenburg Middle School. Their annual field trip. A mob of kids roaming around DC. Maybe somebody saw something."

"Which brings up the obvious question," Breeland said. "Why was Pete Duffy in DC?"

"Too late to worry about that," Mr. Nance said. "Don't follow this kid and don't approach him. But keep an eye on him."

# Chapter 14

Theo was leaving school on a Wednesday afternoon when his pal Woody stopped him at the bike rack. Woody was obviously worried about something. He said, "Say, Theo, you know the judge in Animal Court, don't you?"

It was a loaded question, and Theo immediately wondered what mischief Woody had been up to. He was a good kid and Theo liked and trusted him, but his family was a bit on the rough side and Woody was always either in trouble or close to it. "Sure. What's up?"

"Well," Woody said, glancing around as if the police might be listening, "I have to be in court tomorrow afternoon. My brother Evan and I are being accused of something."

Theo slowly got off his bike, hit the kickstand, and said, "Okay, what are you accused of?"

"My mom and stepdad don't know about this, Theo, and I'd like to keep it quiet." Woody's home life was unsettled. His mother had been married at least twice and her current husband traveled a lot. Woody's father was a stonemason who lived in town with another wife and some small children. An older brother had been in trouble with the law. He asked, "If you go to Animal Court, do you have to tell your parents?"

"Not always," Theo said. He almost added that it's always best to tell your parents, but then he often kept secrets from his. "What's happened?"

"Have you ever heard of fainting goats?"

"Fainting goats?"

"Yes. Fainting goats."

"No. I've never heard of fainting goats."

"Well, it's a long story."


The following afternoon, Theo was sitting next to Woody and Evan in a small, cramped room in the basement of the Strattenburg County Courthouse, waiting for Judge Sergio Yeck to assume the bench and call things to order. They were in folding chairs behind a folding table, and behind them were several other people, including Chase, Aaron, and Brandon, all there out of curiosity. Across the aisle sat an angry man named Marvin Tweel. He was a farmer dressed in his work clothes—faded denim overalls, plaid shirt, and steel-toed boots with mud caked permanently on the soles and heels. Behind him were several people, part of the usual Animal Court crowd of folks trying to rescue unleashed dogs that had been picked up by the town's rather aggressive dogcatcher.

At four p.m., Judge Yeck walked through a rear door and took his seat at the bench. As always, he was wearing jeans, cowboy boots, and an old sports coat. As usual, he seemed bored with what he was doing. He was the lowest-ranking judge in town; in fact, he was the only lawyer who would handle the part-time job. Animal Court got little respect. Theo, though, loved it because there were few rules and no lawyers were required. Anyone, including a thirteen-year-old who thought he was a lawyer, could appear on behalf of a client.

"Hello, Theo," Judge Yeck said. "How are your folks?"

"They're doing fine, thanks, Judge."

Yeck looked at a sheet of paper and said, "All right, our first case is Mr. Marvin Tweel versus Woody and Evan Lambert." He looked at the farmer and said, "Are you Mr. Tweel?"

Mr. Tweel stood and said, "Yes, sir."

"Welcome to Animal Court, sir. You may keep your seat. Things are real informal in here." Mr. Tweel nodded awkwardly and sat down. He was obviously nervous and out of place. Judge Yeck looked at Theo and said, "I take it you represent the Lambert brothers."

"Yes, sir."

"All right. Mr. Tweel, you are the complaining party, so you go first."

Mr. Tweel said, "Well, uh, Your Honor, do I need a lawyer? If they got one, do I need one?"

"No, sir, not in this court. And Mr. Boone here is not a real lawyer, not yet anyway. He's more like a legal adviser."

"Do I need a legal adviser like him?"

"No, sir, you certainly do not. Proceed with your story."

Satisfied and more at ease, Mr. Tweel began: "Well, Judge, you see I have a small farm just south of town, and I raise and sell a certain breed of goats that some people enjoy as pets. Others raise them for meat and cashmere. They're not your typical goats. They're much smaller and easier to care for. They're called myotonic goats, on account of a muscle condition known as myotonia congenita. Now that's about all I know when it comes to the science, but one aspect of this condition is that their muscles freeze when they panic and they get all stiff and frozen, then they fall over with their legs straight out. That's why they are better known as fainting goats. They don't really faint, they remain conscious, but they're out of it for about ten seconds. Then they get up and everything's okay. It's just a muscle condition, nothing to do with the brain or anything."

"Fainting goats?" Judge Yeck said.

"Yes, sir. They're pretty well known in the goat world."

"Well, excuse me. So what's your complaint about?"

Mr. Tweel glared at Woody and Evan and continued: "Well, late Monday afternoon, I was in the house reading the newspaper when my wife sticks her head in the den and says there's a commotion down at the goat shed. It's about a hundred yards behind the house, so I head down there. As I get close, I hear somebody laughing. Somebody's on my property, so I step into my toolshed and grab my twelve gauge. When I get closer to the goat shed, I see these two boys here messing with my goats. I watch 'em for a few minutes. One is on one end of the goat pen, and the other is leaning on a fence taking a video. One—and I can't tell them apart—jumps out from behind a water trough, claps his hands real loud, yells at my goats as he lunges at them, then cracks up laughing when they faint. When the goats get up, they run away, and he chases them, yelling like an idiot until he corners a couple, lunges at them again, and howls when they go down."

Judge Yeck was amused. He looked at Theo and said, "So we have this on video?"

Theo nodded. Yes.

"How many goats were in the pen?" Judge Yeck asked.

"Eleven."

"Please continue."

"And then, and this is what really ticks me off, when things get real still, one of the boys lights a firecracker and tosses it at the goats. Bam! All eleven go down, stiff-legged, like they're dead. At that point, the boys start running, but I'm right on them. They see my shotgun, and they decide their fun and games are over. They're lucky I didn't shoot them."

"Did the goats get up?" Judge Yeck asked.

"Yes, sir, they did, but here's the bad part. About an hour after I get rid of the boys, after I get their names and address, I go back down to the goat pen to check on things. That's when I saw that Becky was dead."

"Who's Becky?"

Mr. Tweel picked up two enlarged photos. He handed one to the judge and one to Theo. It was a fluffy white goat, lying on its side, either in the process of fainting, or in fact dead.

"That's Becky," Mr. Tweel said, his voice suddenly weaker. They looked at him and realized his eyes were moist.

"How old was Becky?" Judge Yeck asked.

"She was four, Judge. I was there when she was born. Probably the sweetest goat I've ever had." He wiped his cheeks with the back of his hand. In an ever-weaker voice, he went on, "She was perfectly healthy. I kept her because she was a good breeder. Now she's gone."

"Are you accusing Woody and Evan Lambert of killing your goat?" Judge Yeck asked.

"She was fine and dandy until they came along. I don't make my goats faint. Some people do, I guess, for fun and sport. Not me. These boys scared 'em to death at first, then I think that firecracker really upset them. Yes, sir, I think these boys killed Becky."

"How much was she worth?"

"Four hundred dollars on the market, but to me she was worth more because she was such a good mare." Mr. Tweel was regaining his composure.

Judge Yeck paused for a long time, and finally said, "Anything else, Mr. Tweel?"

He shook his head. No.

"Theo."

Theo, who'd spent Wednesday night outlining his arguments and had thought of little else all day, began by stating the obvious. "Well, Judge, of course my clients were wrong to be there. It's not their property. They were clearly trespassing and should be punished for that. But there was no intent to do anything wrong. Look, fainting goats are famous because they faint. Mr. Tweel just said that a lot of owners make their goats faint for the fun of it. Go online and check out YouTube. There are dozens of videos of people who own these goats jumping and yelling and springing up with big umbrellas and such, all in an effort to frighten the goats so they'll do what they're expected to do—to faint! That's all."

"But your clients didn't own the goats," Judge Yeck interrupted.

"No, Judge, of course they did not. Again, they should not have been there."

"And they made a video?"

"Yes, sir."

"To post on YouTube, I presume."

"Yes, sir."

"Do you have it?"

"Yes, sir."

"All right. Let's roll the tape."

Theo knew the video would be shown, and he was prepared. It was hilarious and he planned to use it anyway. Some humor might soften up Judge Yeck and show that making a fainting goat faint was harmless.

He had loaded the video into his laptop and wired it to a larger screen. He placed it on a folding table near Judge Yeck and hit a button. Everyone in the courtroom squeezed closer to the table.

The video: a fenced-in pen attached to a shed; a herd of eleven smallish goats, some black, some white, all with large bug-like eyes protruding from sockets, and all obviously minding their own business. Suddenly, Evan Lambert jumps from behind a water trough, yelling and clapping his hands, whooping and lunging at the startled and unsuspecting goats; several go stiff-legged and keel over; others go scurrying about as Evan gives chase, still yelping like an maniac, but also laughing. He zeroes in on one of the goats and stalks it until it decides life might be safer if it just faints; down it goes; others get up, baying at one another in chaotic frenzy; Evan continues tormenting them while, from behind the camera, Woody can be heard laughing uncontrollably.

It was indeed funny, and most of the people in the courtroom could not contain their laughter. In particular, Woody, Evan, Chase, Aaron, and Brandon were in stitches. Theo, the lawyer, managed to watch it with a straight face, partly because he had already seen it many times. Judge Yeck was amused. Mr. Tweel was not.

The video: During a lull in the action, the goats—all

standing now—bunch together as if looking for safety while Evan fishes something out of his pocket. The firecracker. He grins at the camera, lights the firecracker, tosses it near the herd of rattled goats; sounds like a cannon, and all eleven hit the ground, their short little legs stiff as poles. Evan doubles over in a fit of laughter. Woody is heard roaring again.

End of video.

Everyone inched back to their seats. Judge Yeck waited for quiet and took a deep breath. Finally, "Proceed, Mr. Boone."

"I would like for Evan Lambert to make a statement," Theo said.

"Very well."

Evan sat up straight and cleared his throat. He was fifteen but no taller than his younger brother. All humor had vanished and Evan was unsure of himself. He said, "Well, Judge, like Theo said, we shouldn't have been there. It was my idea. I saw a YouTube video last week, and so Woody and I started looking for fainting goats. We looked in the Yellow Pages and found goat farms, then we found Mr. Tweel's place. All we wanted to do was see if the goats would really faint. You know how it is—you can't believe everything you see on the Internet, and so we were just having some fun. That's all."

"Did you post the video?" Judge Yeck asked.

"No, sir. Mr. Tweel said he would shoot us if we did."

"And I will!" Mr. Tweel growled from twenty feet away.

"Enough of that," Judge Yeck said. "Theo."

"Yes, sir, and I'd like for my client Woody Lambert to make a statement."

Woody was cockier than his big brother and was really not remorseful. Theo had cautioned him that any brash talk would hurt their cause. Act like you're sorry, Theo had warned him more than once.

Woody began, "Well, sure, we're real sorry about this. We didn't intend to hurt anybody, or any goat. Did you know, Judge, that they have a fainting goat festival every year down in Tennessee? I swear. Folks take their goats to the festival and for three days make 'em faint. I think they even give prizes. So what we did was not that bad. But, I agree, we were wrong."

"What about Becky?" the judge asked.

"Who?"

"The dead goat."

"Oh, that one," Woody replied. "Look, Judge, when we left there, after a long talk with Mr. Tweel, all his goats were fine. We didn't kill one. If one died later, I don't see how you can blame that on us."

"You gave her a heart attack," Mr. Tweel said. "Just as sure as I'm sitting here."

Theo said, "But there's no way to prove that, Judge, short

of an autopsy. That's the only way to prove what caused her death."

"You want to do an autopsy on a goat?" Judge Yeck asked, his eyebrows arched as high as possible.

"No, I didn't say that, Judge. That would cost more than she's worth."

Judge Yeck scratched his stubble and seemed to be deep in thought. After a pause he said, "You have to admit, Theo, that it looks pretty suspicious. The goats were fine until a firecracker went off and shocked them to the ground."

"They just fainted, Judge, then, they got back to their feet and forgot about it."

"How do you know they forgot about it?"

"Uh, well, I guess I really don't."

"Be careful what you say, Theo," Judge Yeck lectured. "Lawyers have a way of overstating their case."

"Sorry, Judge, but it's going overboard to accuse my clients of killing a goat. Under our statutes killing a farm animal is a felony that carries a punishment of up to five years in jail. Do you really think Woody and Evan deserve five years in jail?"

Woody glared at him as if to say, "Why'd you bring that up?"

Evan looked at him as if to say, "Way to go, super lawyer."

Judge Yeck looked at Mr. Tweel and asked, "Do you want these boys to go to jail?"

Mr. Tweel shot back, "Wouldn't bother me."

Judge Yeck looked at the Lambert brothers and asked, "Do your parents know about this?"

Both shook their heads emphatically. No. Evan said, "We'd like to keep this away from our parents. They have enough problems."

Judge Yeck scribbled some notes on a legal pad. The courtroom was silent as everyone took a deep breath. Since Theo had been there many times, he knew the judge was looking for a compromise, and that he might appreciate some help. He said, "Judge, if you don't mind, may I offer a suggestion?"

"Sure, Theo."

"Well, it's a bit extreme to talk about jail time. My clients are in school, and throwing them in jail doesn't help anything. And since their parents are not involved and they don't have any money to pay a fine, for trespassing, perhaps they could be sentenced to a few hours of labor on Mr. Tweel's farm."

Mr. Tweel blurted, "I don't want 'em on my farm. My goats'll never be the same."

Theo looked at Woody, and, as instructed, he stood and said, "Mr. Tweel, my brother and I are very sorry for what happened. We were wrong to go onto your property, and we realize we're guilty of trespassing. We were just having some fun and didn't mean to do any harm. We apologize and we'd like to do whatever you want to make things right."

Sincere apologies went a long way in Judge Yeck's courtroom.

Mr. Tweel was really a nice man with a big heart. How could you raise fainting goats and not have a lighthearted view of the world? But he kept a grim face and stared at the floor. Woody sat down.

Judge Yeck looked at Mr. Tweel and asked, "How big is your farm?"

"Two hundred acres."

"Well, I was raised on a farm, and I know that there's always brush to be cleared and firewood to be cut. Surely you can find some hard labor for these boys, something far away from the goat pen."

Mr. Tweel began nodding and almost smiled, as if he just thought of some nasty job on the farm he'd been neglecting for years. He said, "I suppose so."

Judge Yeck said, "So here's what we'll do. I find both of you guilty of trespassing, but there will be no record of your conviction. Since you have no money I will not order you to pay a fine. Your sentence will be twenty hours of labor, each,

on Mr. Tweel's farm over the next month. If you fail to show
up or fail to do what he tells you to do, then we'll meet back
here again and I will not be in a good mood. And stay away
from the goats. Fair enough, Mr. Tweel?"

"I suppose."

"Any questions, Theo?"

"No, sir."

"All right. Next case."

# PART TWO

**THE RETRIAL**

# Chapter 15

Theo awoke on Monday morning to the sounds of thunder and rain hitting his bedroom window. It was dark outside, too dark to be awake, but then he had slept little. He stared at the ceiling, lost in a world of heavy thinking, when he realized something was moving beside his bed. "All right," he said, and moved over so Judge could crawl into the bed. Judge did not like thunder and felt safer under the covers than under the bed.

How would the bad weather affect the trial? Theo wasn't sure. It might keep some spectators away, but that was doubtful. The courtroom would be packed. The town had talked of little else since the day Pete Duffy had been captured in DC.

Would Theo be in the courtroom? That was the big question. Mr. Mount had asked Mrs. Gladwell, the principal, if his class could attend the opening day, same as the last time, but the request had been denied. The boys had other classes, other obligations, and it wasn't fair to allow one homeroom so much time out of school. This had really irritated Theo, and Mr. Mount as well, but there was nothing they could do.

The second murder trial of Pete Duffy was even bigger than the first. Why couldn't Mrs. Gladwell understand this? The boys would learn far more in the courtroom than they would suffering through yet another day of Spanish or Chemistry. Once it became apparent that they could not attend as a group, Theo began scheming of ways to get himself excused from school. He had thought about getting sick again, and not just his usual hacking cough or upset stomach or fever caused by placing a hand towel on the furnace vent and then draping it across his forehead. None of those would work, mainly because his parents had seen them so often. He had Googled flu symptoms, and strep throat, and whooping cough, even appendicitis, but realized those afflictions were too serious to fake. Besides, his mother would insist that he stay in bed for days. He'd thought about appealing to Judge Henry Gantry, a close ally, and trying to convince him that he, Theo, was actually *needed* in the courtroom. Maybe he could be useful in some way. He had talked to Ike about a scheme whereby Ike would check him out of school to attend a funeral, but remembered that that trick had already been used. Finally, he had convinced Mr. Mount to intervene and write a request that Theo be allowed to watch the first day so he could report everything back to their Government class. Mrs. Gladwell had reluctantly said yes, but only if Theo's parents agreed.

And that's where he hit a wall. His parents were of the opinion that he had missed too many classes already. Usually they split; if one said yes the other said no, and vice versa. But this time they remained united and Theo, so far, had been unable to persuade them.

He could not imagine missing the trial.

The rain stopped and the sky began to lighten. He showered, dressed, brushed his teeth, studied his thick braces, and finally went downstairs for the final round of battle. His parents were at the kitchen table drinking coffee and reading the newspaper. His father was dressed in his usual dark suit. His mother was still in her pajamas and bathrobe. The air seemed tense. Everybody said good morning, and Theo sat in a chair, waiting. They seemed not to notice him.

After a few awkward minutes, his mother said, "Aren't you eating breakfast, Theo?"

"No," he replied abruptly.

"And why not?"

"I'm on a hunger strike."

His father shrugged, glanced at him with a quick grin, and returned to his newspaper. Starve if you want to, son.

"And why are you on a hunger strike?" his mother asked.

"Because you're not being fair, and I don't like the injustice of it."

"We've had this discussion," his father said without taking his eyes off the newspaper. Theo was often amazed at how much time his parents spent reading the local paper. Did Strattenburg really have so much fascinating news?

His mother said, "Injustice is a pretty strong word, Teddy."

Theo replied, "Please don't call me Teddy. I'm too old for that." It sounded far too harsh and she looked at him sadly. His father shot him a hard look. A tense moment or two passed as Theo twiddled his thumbs and Judge looked up, obviously starving.

His father turned a page and finally asked, "And how long will this hunger strike last?"

"Until the trial is over."

"And what about Judge? Have you discussed it with him?"

"Yes, we had a long talk," Theo said. "He said he'd rather not take part."

"That's good to hear." His father lowered the newspaper and looked at Theo. "So let me get this straight. Tonight we're going to Robilio's, your favorite Italian restaurant. And I'll probably order either the spaghetti and meatballs or the ravioli stuffed with spinach and veal, after, of course, we start with mozzarella and roasted tomatoes. Your mom will probably get the seafood capellini, or maybe the grilled eggplant. They'll serve us a basket of their famous garlic bread. We may even have their famous tiramisu for dessert. And the entire time you'll be sitting there watching us eat, smelling the garlic bread, looking at trays of delicious food being hustled about by the waiters, and doing nothing but sipping from a glass of ice water. Is that what you're telling us, Theo?"

Theo was suddenly starving. His mouth was watering. His stomach was aching. He could almost smell the delicious aromas that hit him every Monday night when he walked in the door of Robilio's. But he managed to say, "You got it."

"Don't be silly, Theo," his mother said.

His father said, "Think of the cash we'll save. Ice water is free at Robilio's. And all that lunch money."

Judge reached up with a paw and raked it across Theo's leg as if to say, "Hey, buddy. I'm not on strike."

Theo slowly got up and opened the refrigerator. He pulled out a bottle of whole milk—neither he nor Judge could stand skim—and got the Cheerios from the pantry. As he was pouring the cereal into a bowl, he saw something important. His father lowered the newspaper just an inch or so, just enough to make eye contact with his mother, and gave her a wicked grin.

The fix was in. They were playing games.

Theo placed the bowl on the floor and resumed his seat at the table, starving. Things were too quiet, and he decided to start another serious discussion. What did he have to lose? "So, again, I don't see any harm in allowing me to watch the opening day of the trial. Both of you know it's the biggest trial in the history of Strattenburg, probably the biggest trial we'll ever see, and it's just not fair to make me skip it. The way I see things, I'm sort of involved in this case because if it weren't for me, we wouldn't even be talking about a trial. Pete Duffy would be in South America and the police would never find him. An accused murderer gone free. But no, thanks to me and my keen powers of observation, and my amazing ability to recognize fugitives, not once but twice, we, the people of this town and of Stratten County, are about

to witness our judicial system in action. Thanks to me. Plus,
I know more about this case than almost anybody. I tracked
down Bobby Escobar, the prosecution's star witness." His
throat tightened and for a split second his lip quivered. He
would not, however, give them the satisfaction of watching
him crack up. "It's just not fair. That's all I can say. I really
think you guys should reconsider."

He folded his hands and stared at the table. They
were lost in the newspaper and seemed not to hear him.
Finally, his mother said, "Woods, do you think we should
reconsider?"

"Fine by me."

She looked at Theo and gave him one of those big,
motherly smiles that made everything warm and happy.
"Okay, Theo, we've reconsidered. But only for today. Deal?"

Theo was thrilled, but he had the presence of mind
not to agree to any deal. He knew he would be in the
courtroom later in the week when Bobby Escobar testified,
but he hadn't figured out how exactly. He jumped to his feet,
hugged his mother, said thanks a dozen times, and went for
the Cheerios.

"I assume the hunger strike is over," his father said.

"You got it," Theo said. And it had worked. He had never
used the threat of a hunger strike to outflank his parents,

but he had just added it to his bag of tricks. One of the great advantages of being an only child was that his parents didn't have to worry about making a bunch of silly rules for the other kids to follow. They could be more flexible, and Theo knew how to work them.

# Chapter 16

At eight thirty, Theo was sitting at his desk in Mr. Mount's homeroom, staring at the clock, watching the second hand slowly sweep through its rotation, waiting for the bell that would begin the day. He had arrived early and had tried unsuccessfully to convince Mr. Mount that he should march into Mrs. Gladwell's office and demand that Theodore Boone be allowed to skip homeroom and hustle on over to the courthouse where the courtroom was undoubtedly already packed. Mr. Mount was of the opinion that they had bothered Mrs. Gladwell enough already. Just cool it, Theo.

The bell finally rang and the class came to order. Aaron raised a hand and said, "I don't think it's fair that Theo gets to go watch the trial today and we don't. What's the deal?"

Mr. Mount was in no mood to quarrel. "There's no

deal, Aaron," he said. "Theo will watch the trial today and give us a recap tomorrow in Government. If you don't like that, then you can write a three-page paper tonight on the presumption of innocence and deliver it tomorrow."

Aaron had no further questions or comments.

Mr. Mount said, "Theo, you'd better take off. Miss Gloria has your pass."

Woody and a couple of other clowns booed and hissed as Theo sprinted from the room. Miss Gloria worked the front desk and thought she controlled the entire school. In spite of the fact that she had a thankless job, one that involved dealing with sick students, and students who were not sick but trying their best to fake it, and angry parents, and frazzled teachers, and a tough boss (Mrs. Gladwell), and all manner of stressed-out people, she managed to keep a smile on her face. Twice Theo had given her free legal advice, and he would gladly do so again because Miss Gloria had the power to let him sneak out of school. He might need her later in the week, but for today his early exit had been cleared. She handed him an official pass, one that would protect him from the pesky truant officers who often roamed the city looking for kids skipping school. They had caught Theo twice, but both times he managed to talk his way out of trouble.

He jumped on his bike and raced away, headed for

downtown. The trial would start promptly at nine a.m., and Judge Gantry ran a tight courtroom. Theo was sure all seats had already been taken. Two television news crews had set up cameras in front of the courthouse and a small crowd milled about. Theo parked well away from them and chained his bike to a rack. He entered through a side door and bounded up a narrow stairwell that was seldom used. He said hello to a clerk in an office where they kept the property deeds but did not slow down. He zigzagged through some smaller offices, spoke to another clerk, and found a dark corridor that led to a landing near the room where the jury deliberated. He held his breath and opened a larger door that opened into the courtroom. As expected, a crowd was already there, and the courtroom buzzed with great anticipation. Ike waved him over, and Theo managed to squeeze into a tight spot next to his uncle. They were in the third row behind the table where Mr. Jack Hogan and his team of prosecutors were going about the busy work of preparing for the start of the trial.

Across the courtroom, Pete Duffy sat at the defense table with Clifford Nance and another lawyer. While waiting in jail, the hair he had dyed blond had returned to its normal color—black with a lot more gray than the last time. He wore a dark suit with a white shirt and tie, and he could have easily passed for just another lawyer.

"Any trouble?" Ike asked.

"No. My parents changed their minds this morning."

"No surprise there."

"Did you talk to them?"

Ike just smiled and said nothing. Theo suspected his uncle had made a phone call during the night and convinced Woods and Marcella Boone that he belonged in court.

At exactly nine a.m., according to the large clock on the wall above the judge's bench, a bailiff stood and bellowed, "All rise for the Court." Everyone immediately stood as a few stragglers scrambled for their seats. Judge Gantry appeared through a door behind the bench, and the bailiff continued: "Hear ye, hear ye, the Criminal Court for the Tenth District is now in session, the Honorable Henry Gantry presiding. Let all who have matters come forth. May God bless this Court."

Judge Gantry, with his long black robe flowing behind him, took his place behind the elevated bench and said, "Please be seated." Theo glanced around. There was not an empty seat anywhere, including the balcony where he and his classmates had been sitting during the opening of the first trial.

This trial was different. During the first one, there had been the general feeling in town that Pete Duffy had killed his wife, but that the State would have a hard time proving it. His great defense lawyer, Clifford Nance, would do a superb job of punching holes in the State's case, of creating enough doubt to free his client. Now, though, at the start of the retrial, there was the strong belief that Duffy was guilty of murder and headed for death row. Everyone knew he had escaped. He had to be guilty! Even Theo, who strongly believed in the presumption of innocence, could not force himself to view Duffy as an innocent man.

According to Ike, Clifford Nance had tried valiantly to cut a deal with Jack Hogan, a plea bargain that would allow Duffy to plead guilty to murder and escape and spend twenty years in prison. He was forty-nine years old, and if he survived prison he might still be able to live a few years as a free man. Hogan, according to Ike, wouldn't budge. His best offer was life in prison without the chance of parole. Duffy would die in prison, one way or the other. Ike thought Duffy should take the offer. He said there was a big difference between being locked down on death row and living in the general population of a prison.

Judge Gantry instructed a bailiff to bring in the jury. A door opened, and the courtroom was still as the jurors filed in and filled the jury box. They had been selected the week before in a closed courtroom. There were fourteen of them—

twelve regular jurors and two alternates in case someone got sick or had to be excused. Everyone watched them closely as they took their seats and settled in. Strattenburg was a small city, only seventy-five thousand people, and Theo thought he knew almost everyone. But he didn't recognize a single person. Ike claimed to know juror number six, an attractive middle-aged woman who worked in a downtown bank. Other than her, they were strangers.

Judge Gantry quizzed them for a few minutes. He was concerned about improper contact. Had anyone spoken to them about the case? And so on. Judges always did this and the jurors always said no. But this case was different. Pete Duffy had money—how much no one knew at this point because of all he'd been through—and given his desperate situation he was not above dirty tricks.

Jack Hogan stood and walked to a small podium in front of the jury. He was tall and wiry, and he wore the same black suit every day. He was a veteran prosecutor and very well respected. Theo had watched him many times in court. He began with a pleasant, "Good morning, ladies and gentlemen of the jury." He introduced himself again and asked the members of his team to stand. Hogan was not flashy, but he did a nice job of breaking the ice and getting the jury to relax. He explained that his job was simply to present the facts and let them decide the case.

The facts: Myra Duffy, age forty-six, had been strangled to death in the living room of her home, on the sixth fairway of Waverly Creek golf course. Golf was a crucial element in the case. At the time, her husband, the defendant Pete Duffy, was playing golf, alone, as he often did. Hogan stepped over to his table, hit a key on a laptop, and a color photo of Myra Duffy appeared on a large screen opposite the jury. She was a pretty lady, the mother of two fine young men. The next photo was of the crime scene: Myra Duffy lying peacefully on a carpeted floor in the living room of a spacious house. No blood, no signs of a struggle, just a well-dressed woman seemingly asleep. The cause of death was strangulation. The next photo was an aerial view of the large, modern home sitting on a heavily shaded lot and hugging the sixth fairway. Using photos and diagrams, Hogan walked the jury through the events of that awful morning. At eleven ten, Pete Duffy teed off on the North Course with the intention of playing eighteen holes of golf. He was alone, which was not unusual. He was a serious golfer who liked to play by himself. The day was cool and dreary; the course was practically deserted. He picked the perfect time for the perfect crime.

At this point, Jack Hogan talked about motive. Pete Duffy was in real estate and had made a lot of money. But, the markets had turned against him and he had a lot of debt. Some banks were squeezing him. He needed cash. There was a one-million-dollar life insurance policy on Myra, and her husband was the beneficiary.

With great drama, and with the jurors absorbing every word, Jack Hogan said, "The motive was simply money. One million dollars, payable to Pete Duffy in the event of his wife's death."

Back to the facts: At the time of her death, Myra was preparing to meet her sister in town for a noon lunch. The front door was unlocked and slightly open. The alarm was in standby mode. The time of death was approximately eleven forty-five. Using a large diagram, Hogan explained that Pete Duffy was somewhere near the fourth or fifth hole on the North Course, about an eight-minute ride in a golf cart from their home.

Hogan paused and stepped closer to the jury. He said, "At that point, Pete Duffy left the North Course and sped away. His destination was his own home. He arrived around eleven forty and parked his golf cart near the patio. Mr. Duffy was right-handed, so like virtually all right-handed golfers he was wearing a glove on his left hand. A well-used glove. But as he entered his house by the back door, he did something strange. He quickly put a glove on his right hand. Two hands, two gloves, something never seen on the golf course. He disappeared inside, attacked his wife, and when she was dead he raced through the house, opening drawers and taking such things as jewelry and vintage watches and handguns. He made it look like a robbery, so that we would believe some unknown thief broke into the house with the intent to burglarize it and stumbled upon Myra, who, of course, had to be eliminated."

Another long pause. The courtroom was deathly silent. Hogan seemed to enjoy the drama. He continued, "And how do we know this? Because there was an eyewitness, a young man by the name of Bobby Escobar. He worked at the golf course cutting grass and such, and at eleven thirty that morning he began his lunch break. Bobby is from El Salvador and he is an undocumented worker. He is here illegally, like so many others, but that does not change the fact that he saw Pete Duffy hurry into his home that morning." Hogan touched his laptop and another aerial photo appeared. Using a red laser pointer, he said, "Bobby was sitting in the woods right here, about halfway through his thirty-minute lunch break. From where he was sitting, he had a clear view of the rear of the Duffy home. He saw Pete Duffy park his golf cart, put the second glove on his right hand, and hurry inside. A few minutes later, he saw Duffy emerge, in an even bigger hurry, and speed away."

Jack Hogan walked to his table and took a sip of water

from a plastic cup. Every juror watched him. He stuck both hands into his front pockets, as if it was time for a friendly chat. "Now, ladies and gentlemen, it is easy to criticize, even to condemn, Mr. Escobar because he is not supposed to be in this country. He came here seeking a better life. He left his family at home, and he sends money to his mother every month. But, he is here illegally, and this will be kicked about at length by the defense. They will attack him. He speaks little English, and when he testifies it will be through an interpreter. Please don't allow this to cloud your judgment. He doesn't want to testify. He's afraid of courtrooms and those in authority, and with good reason. But he saw what he saw, and what he saw was an important part of this crime. He has no reason to lie. He didn't know Pete or Myra Duffy. He wasn't looking for trouble. He didn't know she had been murdered. He was simply a lonely and homesick boy who was having a quiet lunch by himself in the woods, away from his fellow workers. He happened to be in the right place at the right time to witness something profound. It takes great courage for Bobby Escobar to come forward, and for him to testify in this courtroom. Please listen to him with an open mind."

Jack Hogan sat down, and at that moment Theo could not imagine that anyone believed Pete Duffy was innocent.

Judge Gantry tapped his gavel and called for a fifteen-minute recess. Theo was not about to risk losing his seat, so he and Ike stayed put. Ike whispered, "Have you heard from Bobby?"

Theo shook his head. No.

# Chapter 17

A month earlier, the identity of Bobby Escobar had been revealed during a closed-door hearing before Judge Gantry. Jack Hogan had kept his name a secret until the last possible moment, but the rules of procedure required that all witnesses be named before the trial. Judge Gantry had delivered a stern lecture: Any unauthorized contact with Bobby would result in harsh penalties. Tampering with a witness was itself a crime, a serious one, and Judge Gantry would not hesitate to punish anyone who tried to intimidate him. The judge's comments were specifically aimed at Clifford Nance and his defense team, and at one point Nance had objected by saying, "Your Honor, with all due respect, you seem to be implying that we would engage in criminal activity. I find this offensive."

To which Judge Gantry replied, "Take it any way you want, Mr. Nance. But no one says a word to this boy, okay? I'll be closely monitoring his situation."

The police moved Bobby to a secret location and gave him security around the clock. He had limited access to his friends and family. He went to work each day at the golf course with a cop in plainclothes nearby.

It took Theo almost a week to find out where he was staying. Julio spilled the beans one day during recess at school. Julio said Bobby was even more frightened and wished he'd never come forward; said he was painfully homesick and worried about his mother back in El Salvador. She was ill and wanted him to come home. He was threatening to disappear into the vast underground that brought him to Strattenburg in the first place. He wished he'd never found the job at the golf course. Theo urged Julio to convince his cousin to stand firm, be brave, and all that, but even Julio was having second thoughts about getting Bobby involved. He said it was easy for Theo to believe in doing what's right and to believe in justice the American way. But Theo didn't understand what it was like living illegally, unwanted, afraid all the time, unable to speak the language, and constantly worried about being arrested and deported. Bobby didn't trust the police because they spent a lot of time rounding up illegals and putting handcuffs on them. Sure, they were being nice to him now, but what about life after the trial?

Watching Jack Hogan, and hearing Bobby's name tossed around the courtroom, Theo was having second thoughts of his own. He was responsible for finding Bobby and getting him involved.

Things would get worse.

When court was called to order, Judge Gantry said, "Mr. Nance, you may make an opening statement for the defense."

Nance rose importantly and strolled across the courtroom to the jury box. As usual, he began with a bang. Loudly, and with great drama, he proclaimed, "Bobby Escobar is a criminal. He violated the laws of this great nation by illegally crossing our border for economic gain. He has been living here, illegally, while enjoying the benefits of our country. He has a job, one to which he is not entitled, while many of our citizens remain unemployed. He has three meals a day, while ten million American children go to bed hungry every night. He has a roof over his head, while half a million Americans are homeless. When he is sick, he is allowed to go to our hospital for excellent health care, courtesy of the taxpayers." Nance stopped and walked to the other end of the jury box. He glared at the jurors, then continued, "Why is he not in custody? Why is he not being deported back to El Salvador? The answer, ladies and gentlemen, is because Bobby Escobar has cut a deal with the police and the prosecution. He's figured out a way to stay in this country, and not only stay here but to live here without fear of being arrested. He has become a star witness in this case. He will take this witness stand, and when he does he will say anything the police and prosecution want him to say. And after he testifies, he will not be arrested, he will not be deported. Why? Because he has cut a deal. In exchange for his bogus and unreliable testimony against my client, Mr. Pete Duffy, he will be treated differently from all other illegal immigrants. He will be given a special status, that of immunity. Immune from deportation. Immune from the punishment that our law says he deserves. He will be protected by the police and prosecution while they scramble around and try to find him a work permit, perhaps even a green card. Who knows, perhaps they've even promised him the fast track to US citizenship." Another pause as he walked to the other end of the jury box. All jurors watched him closely. He spread his arms and said, "Ladies and gentlemen, let's not be fooled by a desperate man. Bobby Escobar will say anything to avoid prosecution. He'll say anything to stay in this country." He looked into the face of each juror, and slowly walked back to the defense table.

That was it! The shortest opening statement in the history of American law.

Over lunch at Pappy's Deli, Ike said, "Brilliant, just brilliant. He zeroed in on the strongest piece of the prosecution's case and destroyed the credibility of Bobby Escobar."

Theo, who'd had a knot in his stomach ever since Clifford Nance sat down, said, "You think the jury will believe Bobby's lying?"

"Yes I do. Clifford Nance will destroy him on cross-examination. The jury is already suspicious. You need to understand, Theo, that immigration is a red-hot issue in this country. According to the experts, we, as a nation, are split right down the middle when it comes to undocumented workers. On the one hand, many people realize that these people primarily do the jobs that nobody else wants to do. But on the other hand, there are thousands of small businessmen who can't compete with the cheap wages paid to illegals. I'll bet that most of the people on the jury know of someone who lost his or her business because they wouldn't hire undocumented workers. They resisted the temptation to cut corners, and they paid dearly for it when they closed their doors. Illegals are paid in cash, and they often earn far less than the minimum wage. There is a lot of anger out there directed at people like Bobby Escobar."

"But Waverly Creek is the finest golf course around. Why would they hire undocumented workers?"

"To save money, and lots of it. Plus, Theo, they don't always know. There's a lot of fake paperwork around. Some employers don't ask questions. Often, the guy who owns the business will hire a smaller company to do the dirty work and look the other way. In Bobby's case, there's a good chance he works for some small-time landscape company that has a contract with the golf course. It's a murky world and evidence is hard to find. It's easy to just ignore things and save money."

Theo, who hadn't touched his sandwich, asked, "Okay, what happens to an employer who gets caught using undocumented workers?"

"He gets busted, pays a big fine. But that rarely happens. There are too many workers and too many employers willing to pay cash and get the cheap labor. Eat your lunch."

"I'm not that hungry. In fact I feel kind of sick. I wish I'd never dragged Bobby into this mess."

"This mess was started when Pete Duffy killed his wife. It's not your fault, or mine, or Bobby's. A crime often drags in innocent people, people who would rather not get involved. That's just the way it goes. If witnesses were afraid to testify, a lot of crimes would never be solved."

Theo managed to nibble around the edges of his sandwich, but he had no appetite.

The afternoon session began when Jack Hogan called the first witness for the prosecution. Her name was Emily Green and she was the younger sister of Myra Duffy. After she was sworn in, she sat in the witness chair and tried to smile at the jurors. She was obviously nervous, as were most folks when they were put on the stand. Jack Hogan slowly walked her through the events of the day when she found her sister dead. They were supposed to meet for lunch, and when Myra didn't show up, Emily began calling. When there was no answer she suspected something was wrong because her sister usually had her cell phone in hand. Emily hurried out to Waverly Creek, to the Duffy home, found the front door slightly open. She stepped inside and there was Myra, lying on the living room carpet. There were no signs of a struggle, and at first she thought Myra had simply fainted, or maybe had a heart attack. She checked her pulse, and when she realized she was dead, she panicked and called 911. As she told her story, she became emotional but managed to keep her composure.

Clifford Nance rose and said he had no questions on cross-examination. Emily Green was excused as a witness and took a seat in the front row behind the prosecution.

Jack Hogan called his next witness, Detective Thomas Krone. After a few preliminary questions, Detective Krone described the crime scene. A large photo was displayed on the screen, and the jurors got another look at Myra Duffy as she was found on the carpet. She was wearing a pretty dress; her high heels were still on her feet. Hogan and Krone went through every detail of the photo. The next one was a close-up of her neck, and the detective explained that as he first examined the body he noticed a redness and slight puffiness on both sides of her neck, just under the jawline. He immediately suspected strangulation, and moments later, when Ms. Green was being tended to by another detective, Krone opened the right eye of Myra Duffy. It was completely red, and he knew at that time that he was dealing with a murder.

Other photos showed cabinets and drawers the murderer had opened, with items strewn about, all in an effort to make the crime look as if it had been first a robbery, then a murder. Missing were some vintage watches owned by Pete Duffy, three handguns from his collection, and several pieces of Myra's jewelry. These items had never been found. There was a photo of the front door, the patio door, found closed but unlocked, the alarm panel in standby mode. Hogan used an aerial photo for Krone to give the jury a clear picture of the Duffy home and its closeness to the sixth fairway on the Creek Course. Other photos showed the front and sides of the house, all heavily shaded and secluded, the point being that the place was very private. A number of fingerprints had been lifted from the doors, doorknobs, windows, cabinets, drawers, jewelry cases, and the antique mahogany box where Mr. Duffy kept his watches. The fingerprints matched only those of the Duffys and their housekeeper. This was to be expected since they lived and worked there, but it also proved that the killer either wore gloves and was very careful, or the killer was either Pete Duffy or the housekeeper. The housekeeper was not on duty that day. She had a solid alibi.

When they finished with the photos, Jack Hogan displayed a large diagram of Waverly Creek and walked Detective Krone through the locations of the Duffy home, the three golf courses, the clubhouse, and so on. According to the computer log in the golf shop, Pete Duffy teed off on the North Nine that morning at eleven ten, alone. The weather was not good and there were very few golfers on the three courses. He was using his own golf cart, as opposed to walking the course, and according to tests they

had performed, he was either on the fourth or fifth hole at
the time of his wife's death. Riding in a cart identical to his,
a person could travel from the fourth or fifth hole to the
Duffy home in about eight minutes.

As far as Detective Krone could determine, no one had
seen Pete Duffy racing from one course to the next in an effort
to hurry home. No one saw him return to the North Nine after
the time of his wife's death. No one had been seen entering
or leaving the Duffy home. No neighbor reported a strange
vehicle near the house, but, then, privacy was expected at
Waverly Creek. They lived behind gates "out there," and the
neighbors were not accustomed to watching the streets. All in
all, it had been a perfectly quiet morning with nothing unusual
reported, until, of course, Emily Green showed up.

Detective Krone testified that he and his team were
in the house for almost ten hours. He was there when Pete
Duffy arrived in a rush around two thirty and saw his wife
still on the floor. He appeared stunned and distraught.

Like all good prosecutors, Jack Hogan was slow and
methodical, but he began repeating questions that sought
the same answers. After two hours, Clifford Nance began
to object, but Judge Gantry was in no hurry. When Hogan
finally said, "No further questions," the judge announced a
fifteen-minute recess.

Theo hated to admit it, but he was getting bored. It was almost four p.m., and school was out. He wanted to find Julio and make sure Bobby was okay, but knew that wouldn't happen. Bobby was being guarded and Julio had little contact with him.

Ike said, "I think I've had enough for one day. Are you staying?"

Ike, of course, had the luxury of watching the entire trial. Theo's time was limited. He replied, "I guess so. Who's the next witness?"

"Well, first Clifford Nance gets a crack at Detective Krone. Not sure he'll get much, but he'll try and beat him up."

"Might be fun. I'll stick around. See you tomorrow."

Ike tapped him slightly on the knee and left. Theo wanted to pull out his phone and text Mr. Mount, but didn't dare. In Judge Gantry's courtroom, anyone caught using a cell phone was escorted out, banned from coming back, and fined a hundred dollars. Not even Theo could talk his way out of such a jam. The phone stayed in his pocket.

Clifford Nance began his cross-examination of Detective Krone with a few simple questions. He established that Myra Duffy stood five feet, seven inches, and weighed 131 pounds at the time of her death. She was forty-six years old, fit and healthy, and had no physical limitations, as far as

Krone knew. She played a lot of tennis, jogged occasionally, and was really into yoga. Pete Duffy was three years older, four inches taller, and weighed 175 pounds. According to his own statement, he exercised little and smoked two packs a day. In other words, she was not a small woman; he was not a large man. She was in better shape than him.

Was it reasonable to believe Pete Duffy could grab his wife, get his hands around her neck, and strangle her to death without the slightest evidence of a struggle? She had no broken fingernails to indicate she resisted. He had no scratches on his hands, arms, or face to indicate a desperate fight.

Yes, it was reasonable, the detective explained. First of all, she knew and trusted him. Thus, he was able to get close to her without alarming her. If he stood behind her, and grabbed her with both hands around the neck, and applied intense pressure for only a few seconds, she would become unconscious. Keeping the pressure on, she would die in about four minutes.

Manual strangulation was a common form of murder in domestic matters, Krone said.

Nance bristled at this, and asked Krone how many similar murders he had investigated. When Krone couldn't think of another, Nance attacked him as an unreliable witness who said too much. The cross-examination quickly spiraled downward, with both men getting angry and interrupting the other. Judge Gantry barked at both and tried to calm things, but the fight was on.

As Nance hammered away, Krone admitted he was no doctor and had no medical training, not even classes for homicide detectives. Krone admitted he wasn't sure how the murderer grabbed and strangled the victim. He admitted Pete Duffy was not thoroughly examined for scratch and claw marks. He said he knew that Duffy was wearing two golf gloves, and said perhaps this protected his hands from her efforts to free herself.

"Perhaps!" Nance roared. "Maybe this! Perhaps that! What if this! Suppose that! Are you certain of anything, Detective?"

The longer they argued the worse the detective looked, and Nance was scoring points by pecking away at his testimony. After an hour of brutal questioning, Nance said he was finished. Judge Gantry quickly adjourned for the day. Everyone needed a break.

# Chapter 18

Late Monday afternoon Theo was in his office, trying to concentrate on his homework, with his dog snoozing at his feet and his troubled mind wandering in many directions. His main thoughts, though, were of Bobby Escobar and the nightmare awaiting the poor kid when he stepped into the courtroom. Clifford Nance would pounce on him like a rabid dog and probably make him cry. He would call him names. He would accuse him of cutting a crooked deal with the prosecution so he could remain in the country. He would tell the jury that Bobby would say anything to save his own skin. There was no way to prepare Bobby for what was coming.

And it was all Theo's fault. If not for Theo, Bobby would

have never been identified as a witness. If not for Theo, Pete Duffy would be hiding in South America and none of this mess would be troubling him.

He felt perfectly miserable and wished he'd never seen a courtroom. For the first time he could remember, the law made him sick. Maybe he'd become an architect instead.

He was jolted from his misery by a knock on his rear door. Judge jumped up and offered a weak growl, but only to show Theo that he was awake and doing a proper job of guarding the place. Judge really wasn't that brave and preferred to avoid trouble.

It was Julio, frightened and unsure of what he was doing. He'd been there once before, but the thought of going to a downtown law office made him uneasy. He sat in the only other chair in the room and seemed overwhelmed.

"What's up, Julio?" Theo asked.

"Well, how is the trial going?" When they first met at the homeless shelter, he spoke with a thick accent. Now, though, the accent was barely noticeable, and Theo was amazed at how quickly Julio was learning English.

"Okay, I guess," Theo said. "They let me skip school today and watch everything. How's Bobby?"

"They got him in a motel in another town, wouldn't tell me where because the police warned him not to tell anybody. But he's really scared, Theo." Julio paused and looked nervously around the room. It was obvious he had much more to say and wasn't sure if he should do so. But he gritted his teeth and plowed ahead. "You see, Theo, Bobby has a friend, a guy he works with, an American, and this guy was off today. He went to the courtroom, sat up in the balcony, and watched the trial. He told Bobby that things are real bad, said the lawyers called him a criminal and a liar and all sorts of bad stuff. This friend told Bobby he'd be crazy to walk into that courtroom. Said the lawyers will jump on him and make him look stupid. Said that the jury is already convinced that Bobby is just another lying illegal worker who'll say anything to help get a green card. Is this true, Theo?"

Theo was immediately tempted to fudge a bit on the truth, to assure Julio that Bobby would do just fine. Nothing to worry about and all that, but he just couldn't do it. "How do you know this?" he asked.

"I talked to Bobby."

"How did you talk to Bobby when the police have him locked away in a motel?"

"Because he has a cell phone, a new one."

"And how did he get a cell phone?"

"The police gave him one. They thought it was

important for him to have one just in case something went wrong. He called me about an hour ago, said he'd talked to his friend, said he didn't know what to do. Are things really that bad, Theo?"

Theo took a deep breath and tried to think of some way to make the truth sound better. "Well, Julio, you need to understand how things work in a trial. I know it's probably confusing, but, no, it's not that bad. In a trial, lawyers sometimes say things that maybe aren't exactly accurate. Remember, Julio, that Pete Duffy is on trial for murder, and he's facing the death penalty, and he has really good lawyers and they're fighting hard to win the case for him. So they'll say stuff that sounds bad but maybe really isn't so awful. Bobby'll do fine when he gets on the witness stand. And without him, the prosecution will have a hard time getting a conviction."

"Did they call him a criminal?"

"Yes, they did."

"And did they say he would lie to get some sort of a deal?"

"Yes, they did."

Julio shook his head in disgust. "Sounds pretty bad to me."

"It's just the first day of the trial. It's gonna be okay."

"How do you know, Theo? You're just a kid."

Theo certainly felt like a kid. In fact, he felt like a stupid little boy who'd stuck his nose into a world where even grown-ups got roughed up.

Across the street and half a block away, Omar Cheepe sat low behind the wheel of an old cargo van, the kind of vehicle no one would ever notice. He was reading a newspaper that partially hid his face, and thin white wires dropped from his ears, as if he were listening to his iPod.

But it wasn't music on an iPod. Omar was listening to every word being spoken in Theo's office. Over the weekend, he and Paco had spent two hours inside the offices of Boone & Boone. The rear door had been easy to jimmy with a thin jackknife blade. The firm had no security system. It was, after all, just a law office with nothing of any real street value to protect. Once inside, they planted four listening devices, each the size of a small matchbox: one in the back of a credenza in Mrs. Boone's office, in a spot she would never see; one between two dusty old law books on a top shelf in Mr. Boone's office; one on top of a thick law book in the conference room; and one on the underside of the rickety card table Theo used as a desk. Each would transmit for about two weeks before the batteries died. If they were ever discovered, chances were they would not be identified as listening devices. And, the Boones would have no idea who put them there. If necessary, Omar and Paco might reenter the offices during the night and retrieve their gadgets. But they probably would not. Why bother? The trial would soon be over.

Vince, the firm's paralegal, had arrived first on Monday morning. As always, he turned on the lights, adjusted the thermostat, unlocked the doors, made the coffee, and gave the place his usual halfhearted inspection. He had seen nothing out of the ordinary, but then he expected to see nothing. The rear door was locked; there were no signs of an illegal entry.

Omar smiled to himself. "You're just a kid," he whispered.

Julio said, "This is all your fault, Theo. Bobby is my cousin and he's a nice guy. He was just having a quiet lunch that day, sitting by himself in the woods, all alone so he could think about his family, saying his prayers, wanting to go home, and he just happened to see that guy in his golf cart. He didn't know a murder took place. He was just minding his own business. He made the mistake of telling me and I made the mistake of telling you, and you got your parents involved, and then the judge. He was so happy when that Duffy guy ran away because then he didn't have to get involved. Just think what it's like, Theo, for a guy like Bobby. He doesn't know what to do. We trusted you, and now Bobby is hiding in some motel with a couple of cops guarding him, just so he can come to court and get ripped up by a bunch of lawyers."

He paused and stared at his feet. Theo could think of nothing to say. A long minute passed and the room was deathly quiet. Finally, Theo said, "Bobby's doing the right thing here, Julio. It's not easy, but sometimes a person just has to do what's right. Bobby is a very important witness, in fact he's the most important witness in the entire trial. No, he didn't ask for this. He doesn't want to get involved, but a woman was murdered by her own husband, in her own home, and he deserves to be punished. We can't let murderers go free. Sure, Bobby was in the wrong place at the wrong time, but he can't change that now. He saw what he saw, and he has a duty to come forward and tell the jury. He has nothing to gain, and the jury will believe him."

Julio closed his eyes and looked as if he might start crying. Instead, he asked, "Will you talk to him? You have a cell phone."

The idea terrified Theo. "Not sure that's a good idea. The judge might think I'm trying to tamper with a witness."

"What does that mean?"

"It's a crime when either side tries to influence a witness. It's called tampering. It's okay for the lawyers to prepare their own witnesses for trial, but it's not okay for someone else to, you know, put the squeeze on them. I'm not sure if it would apply to me, but it just doesn't feel right."

"I don't understand all of this, and neither does Bobby. I guess that's the problem. This is not our world."

Theo stared at a wall as his mind raced in circles. Something told him it was important to get Bobby's phone number. "How's his English?" he asked.

"Not good. Not at all. Why?"

"Just thinking. Why don't you send him a text on my phone, in Spanish of course, and tell him things are not as bad as he thinks?"

"Will we get in trouble?"

*Fifty-fifty,* Theo thought, but then they were not really trying to influence Bobby's testimony. They were just trying to reassure him. And, Theo would have his number in his phone's memory.

"No, we won't get in trouble," he said, without the slightest trace of confidence.

"I've never sent a text," Julio said.

"Okay, just write a short message in Spanish and I'll do it."

Theo handed him a notepad and a pencil.

"What do I say?" Julio asked.

"Try this: 'Hello Bobby, it's me, Julio, on Theo's phone. He says there's nothing to worry about. You'll do fine and you're going to be okay.'"

If given the time, and also a Spanish dictionary, Theo could have prepared the message himself, but now was not the moment to experiment. Julio wrote in Spanish and handed Theo the notepad. "What's the number?" Theo asked as he pulled out his cell phone.

Julio reached into his pocket for a scrap of paper and read from it: "445-555-8822."

Theo punched in the number, the message, and hit Send. He placed the phone on his desk and watched it for a few seconds, hoping for an instant reply.

"How long has he been in a motel?" Theo asked.

"They moved him Saturday. His boss was upset, but the police told him to cool it. Bobby is an important person right now, and the police are being very nice to him."

"I guess so. He's the star witness. He's gonna be fine, Julio, stop worrying."

"Easy for you to say. I need to get home. I'm babysitting Hector and Rita."

"Tell them I said hello."

"I will."

Omar watched Julio get on his bike and speed away. When the kid was out of sight, he removed his earphones, picked up his cell phone, and called Paco. With a nasty grin, he said, "Mr. Julio Pena just left the law office of young Theodore Boone. You're not going to believe this. Our boy Bobby is now hiding in a motel in an unnamed town, cops all around. Can't touch him, but he now has a cell phone and we got the number."

"Beautiful."

"How's your Spanish?"

"What do you mean? It's my native tongue, remember?"

At Robilio's, the Boones settled around their favorite table and exchanged pleasantries with Mr. Robilio, the owner, who waited on them every Monday night. He bragged about the stuffed ravioli, the evening's special, said it was perhaps the best ever. But then he said that every week about every special. After he left, Mrs. Boone immediately said, "Okay, Theo, tell us about the trial. I want to hear everything."

Theo was sick of the trial and didn't want to talk about anything. However, his parents had been kind enough to allow him to skip school, so he figured he owed them a summary of the day's events. He started at the beginning, with the opening statements, and was in full stride when Mr. Robilio returned.

"What'll you have, Theo?" he asked.

"Nothing," Mr. Boone said loudly. "He's on a hunger strike."

"A what?" Mr. Robilio asked in horror.

Mrs. Boone said, "Woods, come on. The hunger strike lasted about ten minutes."

"Stuffed ravioli," Theo said quickly. Mrs. Boone ordered a calamari salad, and Mr. Boone went for the spaghetti and veal meatballs. Mr. Robilio seemed to approve and he hustled away. Theo continued his narrative. His parents were shocked at the comments made by Clifford Nance in his opening statement.

"He can't call Bobby a criminal," Mrs. Boone said. "He's never been convicted of anything."

"Did Hogan object?" Mr. Boone asked. "It was clearly improper."

"No objection," Theo said. "Mr. Hogan just sat there.

"It's gonna be bad for Bobby," Theo said. "I feel sorry for him. And I feel kinda lousy for myself."

Mr. Boone chomped on a slice of garlic bread and, with crumbs dropping from his mouth, said, "Well, it seems to me as if Nance might hurt himself if he attacks Bobby for telling the truth."

"I don't know," said Mrs. Boone. "There is a lot of

resentment toward undocumented workers." Theo could not remember a single time when his parents agreed on anything related to the law. They were soon quibbling over how Bobby might be viewed by the jury. The food arrived and Theo dug in. It was obvious his parents were captivated by the trial, same as everyone else in town. Why, then, couldn't they simply go to the courthouse and watch some of it? They claimed to be too busy. Theo suspected, though, that they were not willing to admit that another lawyer's trial might be more important than their own work. Seemed silly to him.

Suddenly, Theo was not hungry and could not enjoy his food. After he choked down the first ravioli, his mother said, "Theo, you're not eating. What's the matter?"

"Nothing, Mom. I'm fine." Sometimes, when he was starving, she scolded him for eating too fast. Sometimes, when he was worried and had no appetite, she pressed him for details about what was wrong. And when things were perfectly fine, and he was eating at a proper pace, she said nothing.

What his parents needed was another kid or two, somebody else around the house to observe and analyze. When it came to being an only child, he had already decided that the good outweighed the bad. There were times, though, when he needed some company, someone else to get the attention. But then, Chase had a big sister who was thoroughly obnoxious. And Woody's oldest brother was in Juvenile Detention. And Aaron had a little brother who was mean as a snake.

Perhaps Theo was indeed lucky.

Still no word from Bobby.

# Chapter 19

In a motel thirty miles from Strattenburg, Bobby Escobar sat on his bed and watched yet another old movie on television. There was no Spanish-language station, and he struggled to understand what was happening. He tried, though. He listened hard and often tried to repeat the rapid English, but it was overwhelming. It was his third night in the motel, and he was tired of the routine.

There was a connecting door to the adjacent room, and he could hear Officer Bard in there laughing at something on his television. Officer Sneed was in the other room next door. Bobby was sandwiched between, thoroughly protected. The two cops were going overboard to make him comfortable. For dinner, they went to a Mexican restaurant with good enchiladas. Lunch so far had been either pizza or burgers. Breakfast was at a waffle house where the locals gathered and wondered who they were. Between meals, they either stayed at the motel playing checkers or roamed around the town killing time. For fun they coaxed Bobby into repeating English words and phrases, but his progress was slow. The cops were getting bored, too, but they were professional and serious about their job.

At 9:07 p.m., his new cell phone vibrated beside him. A text message in Spanish read: *Bobby, you are a dead man in court. The lawyers will devour you. You are an idiot if you walk into that courtroom.*

He grabbed the phone, stared at the unknown number, and was stricken with fear. No one had his number but the police, his boss, his aunt Carola—Julio's mother—and Theo Boone. He'd had the phone for less than a week and was still trying to learn how to use it. Now, a stranger had found him.

What should he do? His instinct was to yell at Officer Bard and show him the text, but he waited. He tried to calm himself by breathing deeply.

Two minutes passed, and at 9:09 p.m., the phone vibrated again with another text message: *Bobby, the police plan to arrest you immediately after the trial. You can't trust them. They are using you to get what they want, then they'll slap on the handcuffs. Run!*

The Spanish was perfect. The unknown number had the same 445 area code. He panicked but didn't move. He felt like crying.

At nine fifteen, the third text arrived: *Bobby, the police are lying to you, Julio, Theo Boone, everybody. Don't fall for their trick. They care nothing for you. It's all a trap. Run, Bobby, run!!!*

Slowly, Bobby pecked out a reply: *Who is this?*

Half an hour went by without a response. Bobby felt sick and went to the bathroom. He hung his head over the commode and tried to vomit, but nothing happened. He brushed his teeth, killed some time, and never took his eyes off the phone. Officer Sneed checked in and said he was going to sleep. Bobby assured him everything was fine. Tomorrow was Tuesday, the second day of the trial, and they doubted Bobby would go to court. According to Sneed, Jack Hogan still planned to call Bobby to the witness stand on Wednesday. So, tomorrow would be another slow day.

Thanks, Bobby said, and Sneed went off to bed. Officer Bard was winding down in his room, the adjoining door still open. He puttered around his bathroom, put on a T-shirt and gym shorts, then stretched out on his bed for more television. Several times Bobby almost walked into his room to show him the text messages, but he hesitated.

He didn't know what to do. He liked the cops and they were treating him like someone important, but they lived in another world. Besides, they were just regular street cops. Their bosses made the decisions.

At nine forty-seven, the fourth text came through: *Bobby, we know your mother is very ill. If you walk into that courtroom, you will not see her for years. Why? Because you'll be rotting away in an American jail waiting to be deported. It's all a trap, Bobby. Run!*

The battery was half dead. Bobby quietly plugged the phone into his charger. As he waited, he thought about his mother, his dear sick mother. He had not seen her in over a year. His heart ached when he thought about her and his little brothers, and his father and how hard he worked trying to feed the family. He had encouraged Bobby to travel to America, to get a good job, and hopefully send money home.

At ten o'clock, Officer Bard stuck his head through the door and asked, in awful Spanish, if all was well. Bobby smiled and managed to say, "Good night." Bard closed the door, turned off his lights, and Bobby did the same.

An hour later, he eased from his room into the hallway, down one flight of stairs to the ground floor, through an exit door, and into the darkness.

Theo and Judge were sleeping soundly around midnight when a soft noise interrupted the peace. It was the gentle vibration of a cell phone on the nightstand. The dog wasn't bothered by it, but Theo awoke and grabbed it. The time was 12:02.

"Hello," he said, almost in a whisper, though he could have yelled and his parents would not have heard him. They were asleep downstairs, far away, with their door shut.

"Theo, it's me, Julio. Are you awake?"

Theo took a deep breath and thought of all the smart retorts he could serve up at that point, but quickly realized something was wrong. Otherwise, why the call? "Yes, Julio, I'm awake now, so what's the matter?"

"I just talked to Bobby. He called here, woke us up. He's run away from the police. He's scared and he's hiding and he doesn't know what to do. My mom is crying."

Great. Crying is so helpful at this point. "Why did he run away?" Theo asked.

"He said everybody is lying to him. The police, you, me, the judge, the prosecutor. He doesn't trust anyone and thinks he'll be arrested as soon as the trial is over. He says he's not going near the courtroom. He's very upset, Theo. What are we going to do?"

"Where is he?"

"In the town of Weeksburg, wherever that is. He was

in a motel with the police, and he waited until they went to sleep. He says he's hiding behind a quick shop that's open all night, says it's a rough part of town. He's very scared, but he's not going back to the police."

Theo was out of bed and pacing around his room. Still half asleep, he was struggling to think clearly. Judge watched him curiously, irritated that he was awake and ruining a good night's sleep. "You think he would talk to me?" Theo asked.

"No."

"Probably not a good idea anyway." In fact, it was a lousy idea. Theo knew it was time for him to butt out and let the adults handle the situation. The last thing he wanted was Judge Gantry yelling at him about tampering with a witness. In fact, Theo decided right then to forget the trial. Forget Pete Duffy and Bobby Escobar. Forget Jack Hogan and Clifford Nance. Forget everything and just return to being a normal kid.

If Bobby Escobar wanted to vanish, Theo couldn't stop him.

"I don't know what to do, Julio," he said. "Really, there's nothing we can do."

"But we're worried about Bobby. He's out there hiding."

"He's out there because he wants to be out there, plus he's a pretty tough guy, Julio. He'll be all right."

"This is all your fault."

"Thanks, Julio. Thanks a lot."

Theo got in the bed and stared at the ceiling. Judge quickly fell asleep, but Theo was awake for hours.

He slowly filled a spoon with Cheerios, then flipped it, dumping the cereal back into the milk. He took a bite every now and then, but couldn't taste anything. Fill the spoon, then dump it. Below him, Judge was having no such trouble.

Mrs. Boone was in the den, enjoying her diet soda and newspaper, oblivious to the disaster that was about to unfold in the Pete Duffy trial. By now, the police had discovered that Bobby was missing. They had undoubtedly called Jack Hogan, and the entire prosecution was in chaos. What would the courtroom be like in an hour or so? Theo was dying to know, but then he was also determined to ignore the trial.

At eight a.m., he rinsed their bowls in the sink, put the milk and orange juice back in the refrigerator, walked to the den, and kissed his mother on the cheek. "Off to school," he said.

"You look sleepy," she said.

"I'm fine."

"Do you have lunch money?" She asked the same question five days a week.

"Always."

"And your homework is complete?"

"It's perfect, Mom."

"And I'll see you when?"

"After school."

"Be careful and remember to smile." Theo hated to smile because his teeth were covered with thick braces, but his mother was convinced that every smile made the world a happier place.

"I'm smiling, Mom," he said.

"Love you, Teddy."

"Love you back."

Theo smiled until he got to the kitchen. He hated the nickname "Teddy" and mumbled it under his breath. He grabbed his backpack, patted Judge on the head and said good-bye, and left the house. He flew across town and ten minutes later was standing in front of Ike's desk. Theo had called an hour earlier and Ike was waiting, red-eyed and looking awful.

"It's a disaster," he growled. "A complete disaster."

"What'll happen, Ike?"

Ike gulped coffee from a tall paper cup. "Remember Jack Hogan's opening statement, when he promised the jury they would hear from Bobby Escobar, his star witness? Remember?"

"Sure."

"Well, that was a mistake, because now, if Bobby doesn't show, the defense will move for a mistrial, and Judge Gantry will have no alternative but to grant one. A second mistrial, Theo. And guess what? Under our laws, a second mistrial means the charges will be dismissed. It means Duffy will walk on the murder charge. He'll serve a few short years for the escape, but he'll be out soon and living the good life. He'll get away with murder, Theo. That's what's about to happen. It's a disaster."

Although Ike had not mentioned the reward money in some time, Theo suspected he thought about it a lot. He earned a simple living as a tax accountant, but had little to show for it. His car was twenty years old. He lived in a run-down apartment. His office was shabby and disorganized, though Theo loved it.

Ike seemed particularly upset by the fact that a second mistrial was now likely. He said, "They have to find this boy."

Theo wasn't about to tell anyone he had Bobby's cell phone number; not that it would help. Theo was quite certain that Bobby, wherever he was hiding, was not about to answer his phone. Theo asked, "When do they tell Judge Gantry that the star witness has disappeared?"

"Who knows? If I were Jack Hogan, I'd keep it quiet as

long as I could and hope like crazy that they find Bobby. Hogan has a bunch of witnesses he can put on the stand before he needs Bobby, so he'll probably keep going forward as if nothing is wrong. But by tomorrow, if they don't find him, the game is over. I don't know, just speculating."

"And there's nothing we can do, right?"

"Of course not," Ike snapped. "All we can do is wait."

"Okay, I'm outta here. Off to school. You headed to the courthouse?"

"Oh yes. I wouldn't miss it for anything. I'll call you during the first recess."

Julio was waiting by the bike rack. He and Theo whispered for a few minutes as they headed to class. No word from Bobby. He was not answering his phone. Theo said, "I'm sure the police are searching everywhere. Maybe they'll find him."

"You think he's okay, Theo?"

Theo said, "Sure, he'll be fine." But he had no clue.

"I'm sorry I said it was all your fault, Theo. I didn't mean it."

"It's okay. Let's get together during lunch break."

"You got it."

# Chapter 20

At nine a.m., as Theo sat through Madame Monique's Spanish class, he watched the clock on the wall and wondered what was happening in court. The trial was starting its second day. The courtroom was undoubtedly still packed. The jury was being brought in to hear the next round of witnesses for the prosecution. Everything seemed fine. No one but Jack Hogan and his team knew the truth— that their star witness had gone missing. An hour later, Theo was suffering through Geometry with Miss Garman and thinking of Bobby, who was probably hiding in the woods somewhere watching police cars zip around Weeksburg in their frantic search. He had managed to travel all the way from El Salvador, through Mexico, across the border, and into Strattenburg, without being detected. Theo had often wondered how millions of people could enter the country illegally and live and survive. They knew the secrets of moving in the shadows and avoiding the authorities when necessary.

If Bobby wanted to disappear, they would never find him.

There was a ten-minute break between Geometry and Government with Mr. Mount, and Theo rushed to the playground to call Ike. No answer. He was watching the trial, unable to talk or text.

In Government, Theo stood before the class and gave a summary of the opening of the trial. Since the boys had seen the first day of the first trial, they had a hundred questions. Theo gamely went along, answering them all.

At noon, during the lunch break, Ike finally called. He said the morning had gone as planned without a word about the missing witness. Jack Hogan had told no one. Judge Gantry seemed oblivious. However, Clifford Nance and his defense team seemed much more confident than the day before. "They know," Ike said. "Something tells me they know." But Theo wasn't so sure. Ike tended to exaggerate at times.

Theo found Julio and explained what was happening at the trial. Julio suggested they call Bobby on Theo's cell, but Theo said no. "He's too smart to answer his phone, Julio."

The afternoon dragged by, slower than ever, and Theo suffered through Chemistry, study hall, and Debate Team practice. When the final bell rang at three thirty, he hopped on his bike and headed for the courthouse.

It was odd, watching the trial as if everything was fine, but knowing that the entire show was about to come to another shocking end. The jurors listened intently to the witnesses. The lawyers took pages of notes, scanned documents, and took turns questioning the witnesses. Judge Gantry presided solemnly, occasionally ruling on objections from the lawyers. The court reporter captured every word. The clerks shuffled papers and kept things in order. The spectators watched it all, captivated by the drama. The defendant, Pete Duffy, sat surrounded by his lawyers, and never changed his expression.

Jack Hogan and the prosecution team did indeed look a bit frazzled, but Theo could not detect an unusual amount of confidence on the other side of the courtroom. Everything seemed as normal as you might expect in a big trial.

The last witness of the day was a banker. Jack Hogan was walking him through a series of questions about Pete Duffy's loans and finances, all in an effort to prove the defendant was desperate for cash. Thus, his need for the life insurance proceeds. Thus, a motive for murder. Some of the testimony was over Theo's head, and it became quite dull.

As Theo listened, he watched Judge Gantry, and he felt a mix of sadness and anger. He was sad because the judge was presiding over an important trial, thought things were going well, and had no idea serious trouble was just around the corner. Theo was angry because the trial was about to blow up, and Pete Duffy would once again dodge a conviction for murder. He was certain the police were combing every square inch of Weeksburg, looking for Bobby as the clock ticked and a disaster loomed. And what if they found him? Could they arrest him, and haul him to the courthouse, and force him to testify? Theo didn't think so.

Judge Gantry adjourned at five fifteen and sent the jurors home. Theo and Ike chatted for a moment outside the courthouse. Across the lawn, Omar Cheepe was smoking a cigarette and talking on his cell phone. He glared at Theo as he did so. Ike promised to call if he heard anything, and Theo said good-bye. He took his time riding back to the office. He locked his door and lay on the floor, talking to Judge, telling him how awful things were going. As always, Judge listened intently, staring at Theo with eager eyes, believing every word and ready to help. It always felt good to talk to someone, even a dog.

Mrs. Boone was in her office with a late appointment. Mr. Boone was upstairs, smoking his pipe and reworking the language of a thick document. "Got a minute, Dad?" Theo asked, interrupting.

"Well, sure. What's on your mind?"

"You're not going to believe this, but Bobby Escobar has disappeared."

Mr. Boone's jaw dropped. Theo told him the rest of the story, even the part about having Bobby's cell phone number.

It was Tuesday night, and the Boones walked a few blocks to the Highland Street Shelter to visit the homeless. As always, Theo worked the food line, serving hot vegetable soup and sandwiches to people who had no place to go. Many of the faces were familiar, sad folks who had lost everything and somehow survived without a place to live. They slept on park benches, and under bridges, and in cheap tents hidden in the woods. They rummaged through Dumpsters and begged on the streets. The lucky ones, about fifty in all, lived at the shelter, but most would eat their dinner, slowly, and leave to return to the darkness. Some abused drugs and alcohol. Some were mentally ill. Volunteering at the shelter always made Theo stop and remember how lucky he was.

After everyone was served, Theo, his parents, and the other volunteers had a quick dinner in the kitchen. Some of the volunteers began washing dishes and storing the leftovers. The Boones drifted away. Mrs. Boone went to her little room to meet with clients. Mr. Boone set up shop in a corner and began reviewing Medicare forms for an elderly couple.

Theo was tutoring a fourth grader in math when his cell phone vibrated. It was Julio. Theo excused himself and stepped outside where he could talk. Julio explained that he had just talked to Bobby. He was hiding in an apple orchard far from town, in an old warehouse where other undocumented workers were living. The police had stopped by once, but the workers knew how to avoid them. He was in the process of arranging a ride back to Texas where he would recross the border and head home.

"Did you tell him he needs to stay and to testify tomorrow?" Theo asked, though he knew the answer.

"No, Theo, I did not. Bobby's gone."

Later, when they were home and Theo was getting ready for bed, he told his parents about the phone call.

His father said, "Well, tomorrow should be a very interesting day in court."

Theo replied, "I think I should be there." Though he was telling himself he had no interest in the trial and didn't care what happened, he couldn't deny the truth.

"And why is that?" his mother asked.

"Come on, Mom. Why can't you admit that you and Dad and every other lawyer in this town would love to be in court when Jack Hogan is forced to announce that his star witness has disappeared? Talk about high drama. Clifford Nance will go nuts and jump up and down demanding a mistrial. There'll be a big fight, everybody yelling, everybody shocked at what's happening. You know you would love to see that."

"I'm very busy tomorrow, Teddy, and so are you. You've missed enough school and—"

"I know, I know. But school is so boring. I'm thinking about dropping out."

"Might be a bit tough getting into law school if you don't finish middle school," his father observed wisely.

"Good night," Theo said, already headed for the stairs with Judge at his heels. He locked himself in his room, stretched out on his bed, and stared at the ceiling. There was only one thing left to do and he'd thought about it all afternoon. The idea was to send Bobby a text, a final, desperate plea to do what was right. He was convinced he could do it and not get caught. Bobby wouldn't tell anyone; in fact, Bobby was probably racing across the country now, stuffed in the back of a truck full of apples headed for Texas.

Or maybe he wasn't. Maybe he was still hiding, and his

only means of contact was his cell phone.

Theo opened his laptop and wrote a message: *Hi Bobby, Theo here. The trial is almost over. Tomorrow is very important. And we need you to be here. You will be safe and you will do a great job in court. Please come back. Your friend, Theo.*

He pulled up a Spanish dictionary and began translating. Madame Monique always said that language learners make the mistake of trying to translate word for word, but at the moment, Theo had no choice. He tinkered with it for half an hour, certain it was full of little mistakes, then punched it into his cell phone. He hesitated, knowing he was doing something wrong, but sent it anyway.

After an hour of fidgeting and tossing, he finally fell asleep.

# Chapter 21

Theo awoke, well rested and ready for the day. In the shower, he thought about Bobby, but managed to dismiss all thoughts of the trial.

As he was getting dressed, he thought about Jack Hogan, but managed to dismiss all thoughts of the trial.

As he fixed two bowls of Cheerios, he thought about Pete Duffy, but managed to dismiss all thoughts of the trial.

As he was riding his bike to school, he crossed Main Street and saw the courthouse in the distance, but he managed to dismiss all thoughts of the trial.

As he was listening to Madame Monique talk about Spanish adjectives, he thought about his last text message to Bobby. Of course, there had been no response. But he managed to dismiss all thoughts of the trial.

As he was sitting in Geometry, and daydreaming about an upcoming camping trip, someone knocked on the door and it swung open. A grim-faced Mrs. Gladwell stepped into the room, ignored Miss Garman, looked straight at him, and said, "Theo, please come with me." His heart and lungs froze and his knees were weak as he headed for the door. Outside, waiting in the hallway, were Officers Bard and Sneed. Neither smiled, and Theo's hands and wrists froze, too, just waiting for the handcuffs.

Mrs. Gladwell said, "I just spoke with Judge Henry Gantry, and he would like to see you in his office, immediately. He's sent these two officers to drive you over to the courthouse."

Theo couldn't think, couldn't talk, couldn't do anything but stand there like a frightened little boy who really wanted his parents. "Sure," he finally managed to say. "What's going on?"

Oh, he knew. Somehow his two text messages to Bobby had been discovered, and he was about to be charged with witness tampering. Judge Gantry was furious. Clifford Nance was demanding an arrest. His life was over. He was headed for Juvenile Detention.

"Let's go," Bard said. They marched him down the hall like a man being led to the electric chair, or the gas chamber, or the firing squad. Theo was often amazed at how quickly gossip spread through Strattenburg Middle School, so he was not that surprised when several nosy teachers were standing in their open doorways, watching. In the front lobby, some seventh-grade students were arranging art on a bulletin board. They stopped and gawked at the prisoner as he was led away. A black-and-white police car, complete with logos and lights and antennas, was waiting at the curb.

Sneed said, "Just hop in the backseat."

Theo climbed in and sank low. He could barely see out the window as the car began to move, but he managed to glance back at the school. Dozens of students were standing at the windows, watching young Theodore Boone get hauled away to face the fury of the criminal justice system.

After a few minutes of total silence, Theo asked, "So what's up, guys?"

Bard, the driver, said, "Judge Gantry will explain everything."

"Can I call my parents?"

"Sure," Sneed said.

Theo instead called Ike, who answered. Theo said, "Hey, Dad, it's me, Theo. Look, I'm on my way to the courthouse to see Judge Gantry."

Ike said, "Okay, I'm outside the courtroom. There's a recess; the jury is still out. Nothing has happened in the courtroom but I suspect Jack Hogan finally had to admit that Bobby Escobar has disappeared. Things are pretty tense."

*Tell me about it.* "Well, I'll be there in a minute. Guess you'd better tell Mom."

"Will do."

They parked behind the courthouse and entered through a rear door. To avoid everyone, they took an old elevator to the second floor and hurried into the outer room of Judge Gantry's chambers. It was packed with lawyers— Jack Hogan and his gang and the entire defense team. Hogan and Clifford Nance were in one corner, whispering about something that was terribly important. Everyone stopped and stared at Theo as he followed the two policemen to the big door.

Inside, Judge Gantry was waiting, alone. He dismissed Bard and Sneed and said hello to Theo. He didn't seem particularly aggravated, just tense. He said, "Sorry to bother you like this, Theo, but something important has come up. It seems as though Bobby Escobar has disappeared. Do you know anything about it?"

At that point, Theo wasn't sure what was right and what was wrong, but he couldn't change what had been done. And, he trusted Judge Gantry. He said, "Yes, sir. His cousin Julio Pena called me around midnight Monday and said he'd just talked to Bobby, said he had left the motel and was hiding."

"So you've known about this since Monday night?"

"Yes, sir. I wasn't sure what to do. I'm just a kid, you know?"

"Did you tell your parents?"

"I told Ike yesterday morning and my parents yesterday afternoon. We were hoping they would find Bobby and everything would work out."

"Well, they haven't found him. Any idea where he is?"

"Last night he called Julio and told him he was hiding in an apple orchard somewhere around Weeksburg, said he was planning to go back to Texas and cross the border. Julio called me and told me this."

Judge Gantry removed his glasses and rubbed his eyes. He was sitting behind his massive desk in shirt sleeves and a tie. Theo was sitting in a chair across from him, his feet barely touching the floor. He felt very small. "There's something else," he said, removing his cell phone. He found the two text messages to Bobby and handed the phone across the desk.

Judge Gantry read the texts and shrugged. "These are in Spanish. Did you write them?"

"I had help translating the first, but I wrote the second one."

"What does it say?"

"I just told Bobby that today is an important day, that he's needed here in court, that he'll do fine and he'll be safe. That's all. I wasn't trying to tamper with a witness. I promise."

Judge Gantry shrugged again and slid the phone back across the desk. "I'm impressed with your Spanish."

Theo grabbed the phone and felt his entire body relax. What, no handcuffs? No jail? No yelling at me for sending text messages to a crucial witness? He took a deep breath and managed to fully exhale. The knot in his stomach loosened a bit.

"Did he respond in any way?"

"No, sir."

"Have you talked to Julio this morning?"

"No, sir."

"Well, it looks like I'm staring at another mistrial. Jack Hogan described Bobby's testimony to the jury in his opening statement, and now the kid is gone. I can't believe the police allowed him to get away."

"Hard to believe," Theo said, but only because he couldn't think of anything else.

"You'd better hang around for a while, just in case he decides to call. Unless, of course, you want to go back to class."

"I'll stay."

Judge Gantry pointed to a chair wedged in a corner between two heavy bookcases. "Take a seat over there and don't make a sound."

Theo scampered to the chair and became invisible. Judge Gantry pushed a button on his phone and said, "Mrs. Hardy, send in the lawyers."

Within seconds, the door flew open and all the lawyers who'd been waiting poured into the room. Judge Gantry directed them to a long conference table and took a seat at the end. The court reporter set up her stenographic machine next to him. When everyone was settled, Judge Gantry said, "Let's go on the record." The court reporter began pressing her keys.

He cleared his throat and said, "It's about ten thirty on Wednesday morning, and the State has called all of its witnesses, with the exception of one Bobby Escobar, who is not here and evidently cannot be found. You agree, Mr. Hogan?"

Jack Hogan kept his seat. He was obviously angry and frustrated, but also resigned to defeat. "Yes, Your Honor, that appears to be the case."

"Mr. Nance?"

"Your Honor, on behalf of Pete Duffy, the defendant, I move for a mistrial, on the grounds that the prosecutor, Mr. Hogan, promised the jury in his opening statement that they would hear from an eyewitness, a witness who would be damaging to our case, a witness who could well determine the outcome. The jury had every right to believe this; indeed, we all believed it. Since Monday morning, the jury has been expecting the State to put this witness on the stand. Now, however, it appears as though this will not happen. This is grossly unfair to the defendant, and it's obvious grounds for a mistrial."

"Mr. Hogan?"

"Not so fast, Your Honor. I think this situation can be explained to the jury, and the jury can be told to disregard my opening comments. I'm happy to apologize to the jury and explain my actions. Everything was in good faith. We have presented enough proof to convict the defendant even without the testimony of Bobby Escobar. A second mistrial means that the murder charges will be dropped, and that would be an injustice."

Judge Gantry said, "I'm not inclined to agree, Mr. Hogan. The damage has been done, and the defendant has no way to cross-examine the witness. It seems quite unfair to him to promise the testimony of such a crucial witness and then not deliver."

Hogan's shoulders slumped and he shook his head.
Clifford Nance barely suppressed a smile. Theo couldn't
believe his good luck—a ringside seat at the most important
moment in the biggest murder trial anyone could remember.
He absorbed every word without moving a muscle. No one
seemed to realize he was there.

Judge Gantry said, "We'll stand in recess until this
afternoon. The search is not over and I may have some new
information. We'll meet here at two. Until then, not a word
of this to anyone. I don't want my jurors to know what's
going on. Meeting's over."

The lawyers slowly got to their feet and headed for the
door. Judge Gantry motioned for Jack Hogan to stay behind.
When the door closed and they were alone, he said to the
prosecutor, "There's an apple orchard outside of Weeksburg.
Get the police to search it immediately."

Hogan left quickly, and Judge Gantry sat in his chair
behind his desk. He looked at Theo and said, "What a mess.
What would you do in this situation?"

Theo thought for a second. He was struck by the
loneliness of the job, the importance of making decisions
that had such a heavy impact on the lives of so many
people. When he wasn't dreaming of being a great
courtroom lawyer, he was dreaming of being a wise and

respected judge. Now, though, he was having second thoughts. He wouldn't want to be in Judge Gantry's shoes at the moment.

He said, "I like what Jack Hogan said. Why can't you just explain things to the jurors and let them decide the case based on the testimony they've heard? There's a lot of evidence that points directly at Pete Duffy."

"I agree, but if he's convicted he will appeal, and the Supreme Court of this state will surely reverse the conviction. No trial judge likes to be reversed, Theo. That would mean we would have to try Pete Duffy for a third time, and that doesn't seem fair."

"But wouldn't that give us time to find Bobby Escobar?"

"Do you really think they'll find him?"

Theo considered this for a second and said, "No, sir, not really. He's probably halfway back to Texas right now. Can't say that I blame him."

There was a loud knock on the door, and before Judge Gantry could respond, Mrs. Marcella Boone barged into the office and said, "Henry, where's Theo?"

Theo jumped to his feet and said, "Hi, Mom."

Judge Gantry stood and said, "Hello, Marcella. Theo and I are just discussing the trial."

"I heard he was arrested," she said.

"Arrested for what? No, he's helping me consider the motion for a mistrial. Have a seat."

She took a deep breath, shook her head in either frustration or disbelief, probably both, and managed to relax.

# Chapter 22

The police combed through the three apple orchards near Weeksburg and found nothing. Every undocumented worker within five miles had vanished into the woods; there was no sign of them and certainly no sign of Bobby. By noon, they had reported the bad news to the Strattenburg police. They checked on Julio and his mother, Carola; neither had heard from Bobby. They talked to his boss and he knew nothing. The search was over. The witness was gone.

Theo had a pleasant lunch with his parents and Ike at Pappy's Deli. His father suggested that he go back to school, but Theo thought otherwise. Judge Gantry needed him, he explained. He was under strict orders from the court to stay close to the courtroom, just in case Bobby decided to check in. "No chance of that," Ike said, chewing on a world-famous pastrami sandwich.

Mrs. Boone was due in court at one, and of course Mr. Boone had urgent business back at the office. Theo and Ike strolled up and down Main Street, killing time, waiting for two p.m. when the lawyers would meet again and Judge Gantry would do the unthinkable: declare another mistrial.

At one point Theo said, "Say, Ike, do you ever think about the reward money?"

"Sure," Ike admitted.

"What will happen to it?"

"Don't know. On the one hand, Pete Duffy has been caught and he'll serve a few years for escape. I suppose we can make a claim for the money on the grounds that he was found, brought back, convicted, and sent to prison. But on the other hand, the reward offer states that the money will be given to any person who provides information that leads to the arrest and conviction of Pete Duffy for the murder of Myra Duffy. Murder, not escape and evasion. So, it might be hard to collect the money if there's another mistrial."

"Then we're out of luck."

"Looks that way. Have you been thinking about the money?"

"Every now and then."

"Well, forget about it."

In front of Guff's Frozen Yogurt, they passed two of the jurors, faces they recognized from the courtroom. Both wore large, round buttons with the word JUROR across the center, so everyone would know they were important and were not to be quizzed about the Pete Duffy matter.

Ike wanted coffee so they stopped at Gertrude's, an old diner on Main, world famous for their pecan waffles. Theo often wondered if every small town boasted of some dish that was world famous. The place was packed with other familiar faces, folks Theo didn't know but had seen in the courtroom. Everyone seemed to be waiting for two p.m.

If they only knew.

Theo said, "This is where my dad comes every morning for breakfast. He sits over there at that round table with a bunch of old guys and they eat toast and drink coffee and catch up on the gossip. Sounds pretty boring, doesn't it?"

"I once did that, Theo, many years ago, at that same table," Ike said sadly, as if he remembered a time that was far more pleasant. "But I don't miss it. Now it's more fun hanging out in bars late at night and playing poker with shady characters. The gossip is much better."

Theo ordered an orange juice and they killed more time. At one thirty, his phone vibrated. It was a text from Judge Gantry: *Theo, heard anything?*

*No, sorry.*

*Be here in 15 minutes.*

*Yes, sir.*

"That was Judge Gantry," Theo said. "He wants me back in his chambers in fifteen minutes. You see, Ike, he needs my help to decide this very important matter. He realizes how brilliant I am and how much of the law I know, and he has decided to lean on me during this crucial moment."

"Thought he was smarter than that."

"He's a genius, Ike. It takes one to know one."

"So how would you rule in this matter?"

"I would explain everything to the jury, proceed with the trial, and hope the prosecution has enough evidence to convict Duffy."

"The prosecution doesn't have enough evidence. We saw that during the first trial. And if you don't declare a mistrial now, and if there's a conviction, it'll just be thrown out on appeal. You wouldn't make a very good judge."

"Thanks, Ike. What would you do?"

"He has no choice but to declare a mistrial. That's what I'd do. Then, I'd tell the police to give us the reward money."

"You told me to forget about the money."

"Right."

At one forty-five, Theo followed Mrs. Hardy into Judge Gantry's chambers. She closed the door and left. Theo took a seat and waited while the judge finished a phone conversation. He looked tired and frustrated. A half-eaten sandwich was on a napkin in the center of his desk, next to an empty bottle of water. Theo realized that Judge Gantry didn't have the luxury of stepping out for lunch. Some clown would surely ask about the trial.

He hung up and said, "That was the sheriff over in Weeksburg, a guy I know pretty well. No sign of our friend."

"He's gone, Judge. Bobby lives in the shadows, like a lot of undocumented workers. He knows how to disappear."

"I thought your parents were trying to sponsor him and speed along his citizenship requirements. What happened?"

"Not sure, but I think the paperwork got backed up in Washington. They're still trying, but things are moving real slow. Now, I guess it doesn't matter. His mother is sick in El Salvador and he's going home."

"Well, he sure screwed up this case."

"Judge, I have a question. During the first trial, when

Bobby finally came forward, you declared a mistrial. The following week, Bobby went to Jack Hogan's office and gave a formal statement. They used some ace translator, someone who does the Spanish in trials, and everything was recorded by a court reporter, right?"

"That's correct."

"So why can't that statement be read to the jury? That way, they'll hear everything Bobby has to say and we can finish the trial."

Judge Gantry smiled and said, "It's not that easy, Theo. Keep in mind that when you're accused of a crime you have the right to face your accusers, to cross-examine those who testify against you. Pete Duffy didn't have that chance because his lawyers were not in the room when Bobby gave his statement. If I allowed his statement into evidence now, that too would be grounds for a reversal on appeal."

"I guess it takes guts to be fair, doesn't it?"

"Yes, you could say that." Judge Gantry looked at his watch, frowned, tapped his fingers on his desk as if he were in no hurry, and said, "Well, Theo, I guess it's time. You want to stay here or go back to class?"

"I'll stay."

"Figures." He pointed to the same chair in the same corner and Theo reassumed his position. Judge Gantry punched a button on his phone and said, "Mrs. Hardy, send in the lawyers." The door flew open and the room was soon crowded as they all gathered around the table. When the court reporter was ready, Judge Gantry said, "It is now two p.m. and the search for Bobby Escobar has been called off. The court has before it a defense motion for a mistrial. Anything further, Mr. Hogan?"

Jack Hogan reluctantly said, "No, Your Honor."

"Mr. Nance?"

"No, sir."

"All right." Judge Gantry took a deep breath and said, "I'm afraid I have no choice in this matter. It would be unfair to the defendant to proceed without the testimony of one Bobby Escobar."

From his pocket, Theo's phone vibrated. He grabbed it, looked at it, and almost fainted. It was Bobby. He blurted, "Hang on, Judge!"

# Chapter 23

Pursuant to Bobby's request, Judge Gantry, Theo, and the translator drove five minutes to Truman Park and waited by the carousel. When they were in place, he stepped from behind a row of giant boxwoods and walked to meet them. His boots had mud caked on them. His jeans were dirty. His eyes were red and he looked tired. In Spanish he said, "I'm sorry about this, but I'm frightened and not sure what to do."

The translator, a young lady named Maria, passed it along in English.

Judge Gantry said, "Bobby, nothing has changed since the last time we talked several months ago. You are an important witness and we need you to tell the court what you saw."

Maria raised a hand—"Not so fast. Short sentences please." She handled the Spanish, and Judge Gantry continued: "You will not be arrested or harmed in any way, I promise. Just the opposite. I'll make sure you are protected."

English to Spanish, and Bobby managed a quick smile.

News that the witness had been found roared through the courthouse and the downtown law offices. At three p.m., an even larger crowd gathered. Theo and Ike had prime seats two rows behind the prosecution, where they were joined by Woods Boone, who had somehow managed to pull himself away from the urgent business on his desk. As Theo looked around, he noticed a lot of the town's lawyers jockeying for seats.

Pete Duffy was brought in and sat at his table. He looked pale and confused. He chatted with Clifford Nance, who was obviously upset and animated. Gone was the smug confidence Theo had seen only an hour before.

The bailiff called the court to order and it took a few seconds for the mob to settle in. All seats were taken and people lined the walls around the courtroom. Judge Gantry assumed the bench and instructed a bailiff to bring in the jurors. When they were seated, he looked at them and began an explanation: "Ladies and gentlemen of the jury, I apologize for the delay. I know it's frustrating to sit around for hours waiting for the lawyers and me to resolve matters, but that's what usually happens in a trial. At any rate, we are now ready to proceed. The State will call one more witness, a Mr. Bobby Escobar, who does not speak English. Therefore, we will be using a court certified translator. Her name is Maria Oliva—I've used her before and she is very good— and she will be sworn to tell the truth, just like the witness. It's sort of an awkward way to receive testimony, but we have no choice. I read an article one time about a federal court in New York where they have certified translators for over thirty languages. I guess we're lucky here; we just deal with two. At any rate, the testimony will be a bit slower, and we're not going to rush. I ask you to pay close attention and be patient. Are the lawyers ready to proceed?"

Both Jack Hogan and Clifford Nance nodded.

Maria Oliva stood and walked to the witness stand. A bailiff produced a Bible and she placed her left hand on it. The bailiff said, "Do you solemnly swear that you will translate the testimony truthfully and accurately and to the best of your ability?"

She said, "I do."

Judge Gantry said, "Mr. Hogan, you may call your next witness."

Hogan rose and said, "The State calls Bobby Escobar."

A side door opened, and Bobby emerged, following a bailiff. He ignored the crowd, the lawyers, and the defendant, and walked with some measure of confidence to the witness stand. He had been there before. A week earlier, before the trial started, Jack Hogan had brought Bobby to the empty courtroom and put him through a lengthy, grueling dress rehearsal. Hogan had fired questions at Bobby. Maria had interpreted. An assistant prosecutor had played the role of Clifford Nance, and even managed to yell at Bobby. He called him a liar! At first, Bobby had been rattled and uncertain. But as the day wore on, he began to understand the nature of testifying, and especially that of a brutal cross-examination.

When that session was over, Jack Hogan had confidence in his witness. Bobby, though, wasn't so sure.

He swore to tell the truth and took his seat. Maria was in a folding chair next to him, also with a microphone in her face. The courtroom was silent and still. The jurors were gawking, waiting.

Theo had never seen nor felt such tension. It was awesome!

Hogan began with slow, easy questions. Bobby was nineteen years old and he lived with his aunt and her family. He was from El Salvador and had been in the United States for less than a year. He had crossed the border illegally to find work. Back home he had family—parents and three younger brothers—and they were poor and hungry. Bobby did not want to leave home, but felt he had no choice. Once in Strattenburg, he found a job at the Waverly Creek golf course, mowing grass and doing general maintenance. He was earning seven dollars an hour. He was trying to learn English but it seemed overwhelming. He had dropped out of school when he was fourteen years old.

Moving on to the day in question: It was a Thursday, a cloudy, windy day and the golf course wasn't that busy. At eleven thirty, Bobby and his coworkers began their thirty-minute lunch break at the maintenance shed hidden on the Creek Course. As he often did, Bobby eased away from the others and went to his favorite spot beneath some trees. He preferred to eat alone because it gave him time to think about his family and say his prayers.

Jack Hogan nodded to an assistant, and a large aerial photo of the Creek Course's sixth fairway appeared on the screen. Bobby took a red laser pointer and showed the jury exactly where he had been eating lunch.

His testimony continued: About halfway through his lunch break, he saw a golf cart speed along the asphalt path that hugs the fairway, then cut across it to a home that had already been identified as the Duffy residence. A man wearing a black sweater, tan slacks, and a maroon golf cap parked the cart next to the patio, got out, and reached into a golf bag. He removed a white glove and quickly put it on his right hand. There was already one on his left. He walked across the patio, stopped at the door, and took off his shoes. In Bobby's opinion, the man was in a hurry. Sitting under the trees, between sixty and one hundred yards away, Bobby had a clear view of the man and the back of the Duffy home. At the time, Bobby thought nothing of it, though he was curious as to why the man put on the additional glove and why he left his shoes on the patio. Many of the people who lived at Waverly Creek played golf and stopped by their homes for whatever reason. A few minutes passed as Bobby continued with his lunch. He owned neither a watch nor a cell phone and did not know the exact time. No other golfer was on the sixth fairway of the Creek Course at that time. The man emerged from the house, quickly put on his shoes, took off both gloves and put them in his golf bag. He glanced around, evidently saw no one, then sped away in the direction from which he came. A few minutes later, Bobby returned to the maintenance shed. Lunch break was over. The foreman, Bobby's boss, ran a tight ship and made them resume their work at precisely noon. An hour or so later, Bobby and a coworker were working on a sprinkler head near the thirteenth green, and he saw the same man as he arrived at the fourteenth tee box on the South Nine. The man looked around, saw no one, reached into his golf bag, removed something white, and placed it in the trash can. At the time, the man was wearing a white golf glove on his left hand, same as all right-handed golfers. Bobby couldn't tell what the man put in the trash, but a few minutes later he rummaged through it and found two gloves—one for the right hand, one for the left. He explained that the boys who work on the course empty the trash twice a day, and that they routinely go through it, retrieving old golf balls, tees, used gloves, all types of junk. Bobby kept the gloves for a few days. When he realized the man was a suspect in his wife's murder, Bobby gave the gloves to a friend who gave them to the police.

Jack Hogan walked to a small table next to the court reporter and picked up a plastic bag. He handed it to Bobby and invited him to open it and touch the gloves. Bobby did so, taking his time. When he was convinced, he looked up and nodded. "Yes, these are the gloves I found, the gloves left behind by the man in the black sweater, tan slacks, and maroon golf cap." He set the gloves aside.

His testimony continued: Not long after he found the

gloves, word spread through Waverly Creek that the police were swarming around a house on the sixth fairway of the Creek Course. A lady had been found dead! Curious, Bobby returned to the maintenance shed, then eased through the woods. When the rear of the Duffy house came into view, he saw the same man sitting in his golf cart, surrounded by policemen. The man was obviously upset. The police were trying to calm him.

Jack Hogan asked the witness if he'd ever met Pete Duffy. No. He and the workers were told to be polite to the golfers but never speak to them. Another image was flashed onto the large screen, one of Pete Duffy sitting in the golf cart, surrounded by policemen. He was wearing a black sweater, tan slacks, and a maroon golf cap.

Bobby had no trouble identifying him as the man who entered the house at approximately eleven forty-five, or halfway through lunch, and later tossed away the two golf gloves.

With great drama, Jack Hogan, said, "Your Honor, please let the record reflect that the witness has identified the defendant, Mr. Pete Duffy."

"It so reflects," Judge Gantry said as he glanced at his watch. Everyone had forgotten about the time; it was five ten. "Let's take a fifteen-minute recess," he said. Bobby had been on the stand for two hours and needed a break. His testimony was captivating, mainly because it was so believable, but the back and forth between the languages was exhausting for everyone.

"Looks like Henry plans to work late today," Ike said.

"I thought he always adjourned at five," Woods said, but then Woods never spent time in the courtroom.

"Depends," Theo said, like a veteran lawyer.

Pete Duffy stood to stretch his legs. He looked frail and thin and his shoulders sagged. All of his lawyers were frowning. Clifford Nance huddled with Omar Cheepe and Paco, who were seated in the first row behind the defense. Few people left the courtroom; no one wanted to lose their seat.

At five thirty, Judge Gantry returned to the bench, but only for a moment. He explained that one of the jurors was not feeling well, and, since it was late in the day anyway, court was adjourned until nine the following morning. He tapped his gavel and disappeared. Bobby was escorted from the courtroom by two deputies.

Theo assumed he would be taken to a safe place and watched closely throughout the night.

As the crowd slowly filed out of the courtroom, Mr. Boone said, "Hey, Ike, we're having Chinese take-out tonight. Why don't you stop by the house for dinner, and we'll talk about the trial."

Ike was already shaking his head. "Thanks, but I—"

"Come on, Ike," Theo pleaded. "I have a lot of questions for you."

Ike seldom said no to his favorite nephew.

# Chapter 24

The kitchen table was covered with paper plates, napkins, and cartons of chicken chow mein, sweet-and-sour shrimp, fried rice, wonton soup, and egg rolls, all from Theo's favorite restaurant, the Dragon Lady. Ike used a fork and Theo wanted to, but his mother insisted he eat the food properly, with chopsticks. Judge, however, ate like a dog as he devoured two egg rolls.

Ike was saying, "Based on what I've heard, the medical examiner found nothing on the body of Myra Duffy that came from the leather golf gloves. No fragment, no thread, nothing. The theory is that Pete carefully wiped everything off with a towel or something before he left the scene. The left glove, the one he normally wore when playing, was older and well used, and they were able to isolate DNA from some sweat inside the glove. There was nothing from the right glove, probably because it was brand new. He put it on just to strangle her, then took it off."

Mrs. Boone asked, "Does the DNA match Pete Duffy's?"

"Of course it does, but why bother? With Bobby's testimony, you have an eyewitness who explained it all to the jury."

"So the medical examiner will not testify again?" Mr. Boone asked.

"Don't know. He was in the courtroom today, and Hogan might put him on the stand tomorrow. I certainly would, just to be safe. His testimony would add some weight to Bobby's."

"How did Bobby do on the stand?" Mrs. Boone asked.

"Pretty amazing," Ike said.

"Very believable," Mr. Boone said.

"Theo?" she asked.

It wasn't every day that Theo was asked to express his legal opinions to a group of adults, all of whom knew a ton about the law, so he swallowed hard and collected his words. "It seemed to take a few minutes for the jury to get used to the translation, and for me, too. Spanish comes across awfully fast, but then I guess every other language does when you don't speak it."

"I thought your Spanish was pretty good," Ike interrupted.

"Not that good. I didn't understand very much. But after a few questions, I got the hang of it. Maria, the translator, was very good. It was obvious that Mr. Hogan had practiced with her and Bobby. His questions were brief and to the point, and Bobby's answers were also short, but truthful. I kept asking myself, 'What does he gain by lying? Why wouldn't the jury believe every word?' And I think they did."

"Oh, they did," Mr. Boone said. "I watched their faces. They missed nothing and they believed it all. Pete Duffy is about to be convicted."

"What happens tomorrow?" Theo asked.

"It'll be ugly," Ike said. "Clifford Nance will attack Bobby, just like he did in his opening statement. He'll squawk about the illegal immigrant issue, and he'll accuse Bobby of cutting a deal with the State: his testimony against Duffy in return for a promise not to deport. I'm afraid Bobby's in for a rough day."

Theo swallowed hard again and said, "I think I should be there."

Both parents almost choked as each tried to speak first. "I'm afraid that won't happen, Theo," his mother said sharply. She was usually one step quicker.

"You missed school all day Monday and most of today," his father said. "That's enough."

Theo knew there were times when it was okay to push a little, and there were other times when pushing only made matters worse. This was a good time to back off. He knew he couldn't win. It was better to take defeat with some dignity.

As he got up from the table, he said, "Better hit the old homework."

Both parents were watching him suspiciously, both ready to pounce if he dared to mention the trial again. As he and Judge left the kitchen, he said, barely audible, "I think I'm getting sick."

At seven forty-five the following morning, Theo was eating breakfast and reading the local newspaper online. His father had already left. His mother was in the den reading the old-fashioned print version of the same newspaper.

The phone rang. Once, then twice. It never rang in the morning. Theo wasn't about to answer but his mother said, "Theo, would you get that, please?"

Theo stepped to the phone, grabbed it, and said, "Boone residence."

A familiar voice said, "Good morning, Theo. This is Judge Gantry. Can I speak to one of your parents?"

"Sure, Judge." He almost added, "What in the world is going on?" but managed to bite his tongue. He said, "Mom, it's for you."

"Who is it?" she asked, and picked up in the den before he could answer. Theo bolted to the doorway to eavesdrop. He heard her say, "Well, good morning, Henry." A pause. "Yes, yes." A longer pause. "Well, Henry, I just don't know. He's missed so much school already this week, but . . ." A pause as she listened. Theo could feel his heart quicken. She said, "Well, yes, Henry, Theo makes very good grades and I'm sure he could catch up. But . . ." Another pause. "Well, if you put it like that, Henry, I guess it's not a bad idea." Theo was about to jump out of his skin. Then, "A coat and tie. Well, sure. Fine, Henry, thanks. I'll tell him right now." As she hung up, Theo scurried back to his chair, grabbed his spoon, and crammed in a mouthful of Cheerios.

Mrs. Boone walked into the kitchen, still wearing her bathrobe, but Theo ignored her. He was too busy staring at his laptop. She said, "That was Judge Gantry."

*No kidding, Mom. I just spoke to him.*

"And he says he needs a law clerk today in court, says you were very important yesterday, and says you might be helpful today in dealing with Bobby."

Theo managed to look up and say, "Gee, Mom, I don't know. I have a pretty busy day at school."

"He wants you there at eight fifteen, wearing a coat and tie, just like a real lawyer."

Theo bolted for the stairs.

At eight fifteen, Theo followed Mrs. Hardy into Judge Gantry's chambers. She said, "Here he is," and turned around and left. He took a seat across the wide desk and waited for Judge Gantry to finish reading a document. He looked tired and grumpy. Finally, he said, "Good morning, Theo."

"Good morning."

"I thought you would want to be here today. It promises to be rather eventful, and since you're the real reason we're even having this trial, I thought you might enjoy watching it come to an end."

"An end?"

"Yes, an end. Do you know what a law clerk does, Theo?"

"Sort of. I think they do research for judges and stuff like that."

"That's part of it. I use clerks from time to time, usually law students home for the summer. Often they're more trouble than they're worth, but occasionally I'll get a good one. I like the ones who don't say much but are good listeners and watch things closely in the courtroom." He stood and stretched his back. Theo was afraid to speak.

Judge Gantry said, "I was here until almost midnight

last night, Theo, meeting with the lawyers. A lot of stuff
is happening, and I want your opinion." He began pacing
behind his desk, still stretching as if he had pulled a muscle
somewhere. "You see, Theo, Myra Duffy has two sons, Will
and Clark, two fine young men who are in college. I'm sure
you've seen them in the courtroom. They've been here every
day."

"Yes, sir."

"Their father was killed in a plane crash when they were
young teenagers. After a few years, she married Pete Duffy,
and Will and Clark got along well with their stepfather. Pete
was good to them, provided for them, took them places,
and has paid for their college. Of course they are bitter and
broken over what happened to their mother, and they want
him punished severely. But they have decided that they do
not want Pete to get the death penalty. They think it's too
harsh, and they still have some feelings for the man, in spite
of what he did. They've spent a lot of time with their aunt,
Emily Green, Myra's sister, and together they've made a
family decision. No death penalty for Pete. Yesterday, after
Bobby testified, and after it became pretty obvious that the
jury is likely to find Pete guilty, they approached Jack Hogan
and asked him to back off the death penalty. This puts Jack
in a tough position. As the State's prosecutor, he has the

obligation to punish murderers to the fullest extent of the law, but Jack has never asked a jury to condemn a man to death. He also allows the family of the victim to have considerable input into the matter. Last night, Jack Hogan approached Clifford Nance and told him of the family's decision. Hogan also offered a deal—a plea bargain. If Pete Duffy will admit to the murder, the State will suggest a sentence of life in prison, without the chance of parole. LWOP, as it's known. Life without parole. I was notified, and we met here for several hours last night discussing the plea bargain. It means, of course, that Pete Duffy will eventually die in prison, but he won't sit on death row waiting to be executed. It also means that this case will come to an end and the lawyers won't be forced to spend the next fifteen years fighting through the appeals. As you probably know, capital murder verdicts drag on for years. Now, I have to either approve of the plea bargain, or not. What do you think about it?"

"Will Pete Duffy take the deal and plead guilty?" Theo asked.

"Don't know yet. I suspect he had a very long night in jail. Clifford Nance is leaning in favor of the deal, and when we last spoke he had decided to recommend to Pete that he take it. Anything is better than living on death row waiting for an execution."

"I like it, Judge," Theo said. "When I think of the death penalty, I think of serial murderers and terrorists and drug dealers, really nasty people. I don't think of men like Pete Duffy."

"Murder is murder."

"I guess, but Pete Duffy wouldn't commit murder again, would he?"

"I doubt it. So you're in favor of the plea bargain?"

"Yes, sir. I have some doubts about the death penalty anyway. With this deal, the man gets punished, the family is satisfied, and justice is done. I like it."

"Okay. The lawyers will be here in a few minutes. I want you to take your seat over there and stay out of the way. Not a peep, okay?"

"Sure, but would a real law clerk have to hide in the corner?"

"So you want a seat at the table?"

"Sure."

"Sorry. Just consider yourself lucky to be here."

"Yes, sir. And thanks, Judge."

# Chapter 25

The air was heavy with tension as the lawyers filed into the room. Several glanced at Theo in the corner but no one seemed to care. There were far more important matters at the moment. They packed around the long table, opened their briefcases, pulled out papers and notepads, and settled into place. Judge Gantry took his seat at one end and the court reporter situated herself next to him. On one side was Jack Hogan and his gang of prosecutors. On the other was Clifford Nance and his defense team. Pete Duffy was not present.

Judge Gantry said, "Let's go on the record," and the court reporter began pressing keys.

"Mr. Nance, the offer on the table has not changed since midnight. Has Mr. Duffy made a decision?"

Clifford Nance looked as though he hadn't slept in a week. He wore expensive suits and always looked the part of a successful trial lawyer, but now his tie was crooked, his shirt wrinkled. He said, "Your Honor, I met with my client at midnight, and again this morning at six a.m. He has finally agreed to plead guilty and take the deal."

"Mr. Hogan, do you have the Plea Agreement?"

"Yes, Your Honor." One of Hogan's assistants produced a neat stack of papers and everyone got a copy. Hogan said, "It's fairly straightforward, Your Honor."

Theo had heard this before. In fact, his father claimed that when a lawyer says something is "fairly straightforward," then you'd better look out. It's actually pretty complicated.

The lawyers slowly read the agreement. It was only two pages long, and, in fact, fairly straightforward.

Judge Gantry said, "The defendant pleads guilty to one count of murder and gets a sentence of life without parole. He also pleads guilty to one count of escape and gets a sentence of two years, which will run concurrently with his life sentence."

"That's right, Your Honor," Hogan said.

"I have decided to approve this Plea Agreement. Bring in the defendant."

A deputy prosecutor stepped to the door, opened it, and nodded at someone in the reception area. A uniformed officer walked in, followed by Pete Duffy, who was followed by another officer. There were no handcuffs and no leg chains. Duffy was wearing his standard dark suit. Oddly, he seemed relaxed and managed to smile at Judge Gantry. As he was about to sit next to Clifford Nance, he glanced around the room and saw Theo. His smile vanished. His spine stiffened. He took a few steps toward the corner.

Theo knew Duffy wouldn't hurt him, not at this point anyway, but his heart froze for a second. Duffy glared at him and said, "You found me, didn't you? At the airport in Washington. It was you, wasn't it?"

Theo wasn't about to answer, but he returned the glare and didn't blink.

"That's enough," Judge Gantry growled as an officer grabbed Duffy's elbow. He led him back to the table where he sat next to Clifford Nance. Theo took a deep breath.

Judge Gantry said, "Mr. Duffy, I have here a two-page Plea Agreement that I want you to read carefully."

Duffy didn't reach for the document. Instead, he said, "I know what's in it, Judge. I don't need to read it. Mr. Nance has explained everything."

"And you wish to plead guilty?"

"Yes, sir."

"All right. In order to accept your guilty plea, I have to ask you a series of questions."

Reading from a well-used manual, Judge Gantry began the questioning. First, he made sure Duffy knew what he was doing. Had he discussed all the issues with his lawyer? Yes. Was he satisfied with his lawyer's advice? Yes. Did he have any complaints about his lawyer and the job he'd done? No. Did he understand that he would spend the rest of his life in prison? Yes. That by pleading guilty, he was giving up all rights to an appeal? Yes, he understood. That he could never change his mind after he signed the Plea Agreement? Yes. Judge Gantry inquired about his mental state. Was he taking medications? No. Anything that might cloud his judgment? No. Anything that might prevent him from making such an important decision? No.

This began to drag a bit, and Theo had a great idea. He slowly pulled his cell phone out of his pocket, and hiding it behind a leg while staring at the back of the judge's head, sent a text to Ike: *With Gantry now. Duffy pleading guilty!!*

The reply came seconds later: *I knew it.*

Typical Ike. He thought he knew everything regardless of how much he really knew.

Theo was suddenly hit with the horrible thought that he had violated the trust Judge Gantry had placed in him. The judge would certainly want this little meeting to be kept quiet. This was a matter of the most serious nature.

Theo hurriedly sent another text: *Keep it quiet, big mouth.*

Ike replied: *I'm in the courtroom. Everybody knows it.*

That made Theo feel somewhat better. Secrets were hard to keep around the courthouse, anyway, and it was safe to assume the gossip was spreading like wildfire. He wisely decided to stick the phone back in his pocket.

When Judge Gantry finished his thorough questioning, he said, "Very well. I am satisfied that the defendant, Pete Duffy, is fully aware of what he is doing, has been properly advised by counsel, and is not being coerced in any way. Mr. Duffy, I hereby find you guilty of the murder of Myra Duffy, and I find you guilty of escape and evasion. All parties will now sign the Plea Agreement."

As the judge spoke, Duffy sat back in his chair and glanced at Theo. Slowly, Duffy shook his head.

When the paperwork was finished, Judge Gantry stood and said, "Gentlemen, take your places in the courtroom, and I will address the jury."

Mr. and Mrs. Boone were seated with Ike in the crowd, waiting. Everyone seemed to be talking at once, and the large, stately room buzzed in anticipation. When the lawyers appeared from the back, people took their seats. All eyes were on Pete Duffy as he walked to his chair,

offering a fake smile along the way, as if things were just
swell.

A bailiff stood and bellowed, "Order in the Court."
Things were instantly quiet and still.

Ike leaned over to Mrs. Boone and said, "I don't see
Theo." She shrugged. Mr. Boone looked puzzled. The kid
was nowhere to be seen.

The bailiff waited until everyone was nice and settled,
then yelled, "All rise for the Court." Everyone jumped to
their feet as Judge Gantry stepped through the rear door,
his long black robe flowing behind him. And right behind
the robe was his young law clerk.

As Theo stepped onto the bench and saw the packed
courtroom, with everyone standing because of tradition,
and everyone staring up out of respect, he decided at that
instant that perhaps being a judge wasn't so bad after all.
He told himself not to smile; things were far too important
for that.

Judge Gantry lowered himself into his heavy, black
chair, and said, "Please be seated." As the crowd fell noisily
back onto the benches, he pointed to an empty chair next
to the bench and whispered, "Take a seat there, Theo." Theo
quickly sat down. His spot was just a few feet lower than the
bench—more like a throne—and from there he could see
every face in the courtroom. He winked at his mother but

doubted she caught it. He gazed up at the packed balcony, and thought about all his buddies at school, toiling away in class. He noticed a few people staring at him, no doubt wondering "What's that kid doing up there?"

Judge Gantry said, "Good morning. Please bring in the jury."

A bailiff opened a door and the jury filed in for the last time. Theo looked at the defense table and realized Pete Duffy was glaring at him.

*Too bad, Pete. You're headed for a few decades in the slammer. And you're lucky to get that.*

When the jurors were in place, Judge Gantry addressed them: "Good morning, ladies and gentlemen. A few minutes ago, in my chambers, the defendant, Mr. Pete Duffy, pled guilty to murder."

Every juror looked at Pete Duffy, who was studying his fingernails. A few gasps rumbled through the crowd.

Judge Gantry continued, "In a month or so he will be formally sentenced by this court to prison for the rest of his life, without the chance of ever being paroled. So, at this point this trial comes to an end. I want to thank you for your service, for performing your duties as citizens. Our judicial system depends upon the unselfish service of people like you who do not volunteer for jury duty, but give of your valuable time anyway. You have been a wonderful jury, alert, attentive, and willing to serve. Thank you. At this point, you are dismissed."

All of the jurors were surprised, some looked confused, but all seemed suddenly eager to leave the courtroom.

The judge looked at Pete Duffy and said, "The defendant will remain in the custody of the Stratten County sheriff until further notified." He tapped his gavel and said, "Court's adjourned."

As they were leaving the courtroom, Judge Gantry put his hand on Theo's shoulder and said, "Nice work, Theo. Now get your butt back to school."

# Chapter 26

A week later, Theo was in his office, suffering through his homework, listening to raindrops on his window, thinking about how boring life had become since the Duffy trial ended, when his mother opened his door and said, "Theo, could you please join us in the conference room?"

"Sure, Mom." The meeting had been scheduled, though Theo would have little to say. He walked to the conference room, said hello to Ike, and shook hands with Sheriff Mackintosh. Both of his parents were there, and the adults had been meeting for some time before Theo was called in.

The sheriff explained that, in his opinion, Theo was entitled to the entire reward of $100,000. It was Theo who had spotted Pete Duffy, not once but twice. It was Theo who had been quick enough to take a video. He had called in Ike, and so on. It was Theo who had been recruited by the FBI to track down Duffy.

Theo certainly agreed with all of this. His problem was that his parents were getting in the way.

Mr. Boone said, "Yes, Sheriff, we know all of this, and we are very proud of Theo. But, as we've said, Theo has no business with this kind of money. Now or later."

Mrs. Boone added, "And he had some help. Ike dropped everything and went to Washington to help Theo. We think Ike should get some of the money."

Ike wanted a fifty-fifty split with Theo, but he wouldn't admit to this.

Mr. and Mrs. Boone had already suggested that half of the money should be given to Bobby Escobar, for obvious reasons. Without Bobby, there would have been no pressure on Pete Duffy to plead guilty. And, if anyone needed the money it was Bobby.

Mr. Boone suggested that $25,000 should be paid to Theo. The money would go into a trust account for college. Another $25,000 should be paid to Ike, in cash. And $50,000 should be given to Bobby, in another trust account to be handled by Mr. Boone. The money would be supervised by the court and spent wisely.

Theo didn't understand everything about a trust

account. What he did understand, though, was that the money was off-limits to him and would be controlled by his parents. In other words, he couldn't touch it. He wasn't thrilled with the way the money was being divided. He couldn't get his hands on a dime. Bobby deserved something, but half?

However, Theo couldn't bring himself to argue with his parents. He didn't want to seem greedy, nor did he want to take anything away from Bobby.

Ike wasn't too thrilled either, but $25,000 was more than he had a month ago. Two days earlier, in a meeting Theo had not been invited to, Ike had argued with his brother and Marcella over how to split the money. He wanted more for Theo and himself and less for Bobby. They would not yield.

The sheriff asked Ike, "Is this okay with you, Mr. Boone?"

"Sure," Ike said. Whatever. He was tired of arguing.

"And you, Theo?" the sheriff asked.

"Sure," Theo said, though he really didn't have a vote.

On the narrow street behind the office, Omar Cheepe and Paco sat low in a four-wheel drive pickup. On the dashboard was a receiver with the speaker on. As they listened to the

Boones and the sheriff, they shook their heads in disbelief.

"Now we know," Omar said. "I suspected that kid all along, and Pete knew he and his crazy uncle were in the airport. Now we know."

"But it's too late, right?" Paco asked.

Omar smiled and said, "Paco, Paco. Haven't you learned that it's never too late for revenge?"

Even a future star lawyer
like **Theodore Boone** has to deal with
statewide standardized testing—

# the scandal

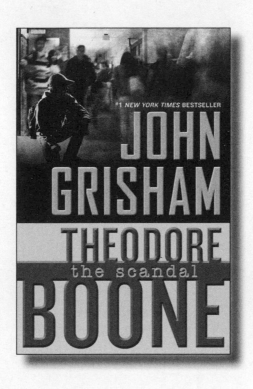

Text copyright © 2016 by Boone & Boone, LLC

Theodore Boone woke up in a foul mood. In fact, he'd gone to bed in a foul mood, and things had not improved during the night. As a few rays of morning sun lit his room, he stared at the ceiling and tried to think of ways to avoid this entire week. Generally, he enjoyed school—his friends, the teachers, most of the classes, debating—but there were times when he just wanted to stay in bed. This was one of those times, the worst week of the year. Beginning tomorrow, Tuesday, and running through Friday, he and every other eighth grader would be stuck at their desks taking a series of dreadful tests.

Judge knew something was wrong, and at some point had left his spot beside Theo's bed and assumed his spot on top of the covers. Mrs. Boone frowned on the idea of the dog sleeping in Theo's bed, but she was downstairs having her quiet time with the morning newspaper and wouldn't know. Or would she? Occasionally she noticed dog hair on the covers and asked Theo if Judge was sleeping with him. Most of the time Theo said yes, but quickly followed the admission with the question: "What am I supposed to do?" He couldn't watch the dog while he, Theo, was sound asleep. And, to be honest, Theo didn't really want the dog in the bed with him. Judge had the irritating habit of stretching himself out smack in the middle of things and expecting Theo to retreat to the edges, where he often came within inches of crashing to the floor and waking up with a sore head. No, Theo preferred that Judge sleep on his little doggy bed down below.

The truth was, Judge did whatever he wanted to do, and not only in Theo's room but in every room in the house.

On days like today, Theo envied his dog. What a life: no school, no homework, no tests, no pressure. He ate whenever he wanted, napped most of the day at the office, and seemed unconcerned about most things. The Boones took care of his needs, and he did anything he wanted.

Reluctantly, Theo got out of bed, rubbed his dog's head, said good morning, but not with as much enthusiasm as usual, and went to the bathroom. Last week the orthodontist had readjusted his braces, and his jaws still ached. He grinned at himself in the mirror, took stock of the mouthful of metal that he despised, and tried to find hope in the fact that he *might* get the braces off just in time to start the ninth grade.

He stepped into the shower and thought about the ninth grade. High school. He just wasn't ready for it. He was thirteen and quite content at Strattenburg Middle School, where he liked his teachers, most of them anyway, and was captain of the Debate Team, almost an Eagle Scout and, well, thought of himself as a leader. He was certainly the only kid lawyer in the school, the only kid he knew of who dreamed of being either a big-time trial lawyer or a brilliant young judge. He couldn't make up his mind. In the ninth grade he would be just another lowly freshman at the bottom of the pile. Freshmen got no respect in high school. Middle school was okay because Theo had found his place, a place that would disappear in a few months. High school was all about football, basketball, cheerleaders, driving, dating, band, theatre, large classes, clothes, shaving, and, well, growing up. He just wasn't ready for it. Most of his friends wanted to hurry along and grow up, but not Theo.

He stepped out of the shower and dried off. Judge was watching him and thinking about nothing but breakfast. Such a lucky dog.

As Theo brushed his teeth, or rather cleaned his braces, he admitted that life was changing. High school was slowly rising on the horizon. One of its most important and unpleasant warning signs was standardized testing, a horrible idea cooked up by some experts far away. Those people had decided that it was important to give the same tests at the same time to every eighth grader in the state so that the folks in charge of Strattenburg Middle School and all the other schools would know how they stacked up. That was one reason for the tests. Another reason, at least in Strattenburg, was to separate the eighth graders into three groups for high school. The smartest would be fast-tracked into an Honors program. The weaker students would be placed on a slower track. And the average kids would be treated normally and allowed to enjoy high school without special treatment.

Yet another reason for the tests was to measure how well the teachers were doing. If a teacher's class did really well, he or she would qualify for a bonus. And if the class did poorly, all kinds of bad things might happen to the teacher. He or she might even be fired.

Needless to say, the entire process of testing, scoring, tracking, and evaluating teachers had become hotly controversial. The students, of course, hated it. Most of the teachers didn't like it. Almost all parents wanted their kids in the Honors classes, and almost all were disappointed. Those with kids on the "slow track" were mad, even embarrassed.

And so the debate raged. Mrs. Boone was firmly opposed to the testing, so, of course, Mr. Boone supported it. The family had talked about testing for weeks, over dinner and in the car, and even while watching television. For a month, the eighth-grade teachers had been preparing the students for the tests. "Teaching to the tests," was the favorite description, which meant no creative teaching was being done and no one was having fun in class.

Theo was already sick of the tests, and they had not even started.

He dressed, grabbed his backpack, and went downstairs, Judge at his heels. He said hello to his mother, who, as always, was curled up on the sofa in her robe, sipping coffee and reading the newspaper. Mr. Boone always left early and joined his friends for coffee and gossip at the same downtown diner.

Theo fixed two bowls of Cheerios and put one on the floor for Judge. They almost always ate in silence, but occasionally Mrs. Boone joined them for a chat. She did this when she suspected something was bothering Theo. Today, she entered the kitchen, poured more coffee, and took a seat across from her son. "What's up today?" she asked.

"More reviewing, more practicing how to take the tests."

"Are you nervous?"

"Not really. I'm just tired already. I don't do well on these tests, so I don't like them."

It was true. Theo was almost a straight-A student, with an occasional B in the sciences, but he had never done well on standardized tests. "What if I don't make the Honors track next year?" he asked.

"Teddy, you're going to excel in high school, college, and law school, if you choose to go there. Don't worry about where they put you in the ninth grade."

"Thanks, Mom." Her words felt good in spite of the fact that she called him "Teddy," a little nickname that, thankfully, only she used, and only when they were alone.

Theo had friends whose parents were turning flips and losing sleep over the tests. If their kids didn't make Honors, the parents were convinced their kids were headed for miserable lives. The whole thing seemed silly to Theo.

She said, "I suppose you know that there is a backlash across the country against these tests. They are becoming very unpopular, and there appears to be widespread cheating."

"How do you cheat on a standardized test?"

"I'm not sure, but I've read about some of the cheating. In one district the teachers changed answers. Hard to believe, isn't it?"

"Why would a teacher do that?"

"Well, in that case, the school was not very good and on probation with the district. Plus, the teachers wanted to qualify for a bonus. None of it makes any sense."

"I think I'm getting sick. Do I look pale?"

"No, Teddy. You look perfectly healthy."

It was eight o'clock, time to move. Theo rinsed both bowls and left them in the sink, same as always. He kissed his mom on the cheek and said, "I'm off."

"Do you have lunch money?" she asked, the same question five days a week.

"Always."

"And your homework is complete?"

"It's perfect, Mom."

"And I'll see you when?"

"I'll stop by the office after school." Theo stopped by the office every day after school, without fail, but Mrs. Boone always asked.

"Be careful," she said. "And remember to smile."

"I'm smiling, Mom."

"Love you, Teddy."

"Love you back."

Theo stepped outside and said good-bye to Judge, who would ride in the car with Mrs. Boone to the office where he would spend his day sleeping and eating and worrying about nothing. Theo jumped on his bike and sped away, once again wishing he could be a dog for the next four days.

Read how it all began in . . .

## kid lawyer

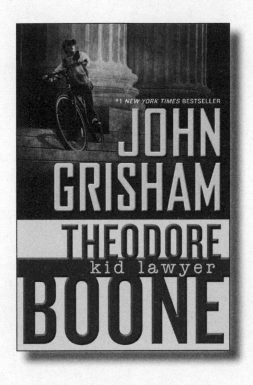

Text copyright © 2010 by Belfry Holdings, Inc.

Theodore Boone was an only child and for that reason usually had breakfast alone. His father, a busy lawyer, was in the habit of leaving early and meeting friends for coffee and gossip at the same downtown diner every morning at seven. Theo's mother, herself a busy lawyer, had been trying to lose ten pounds for at least the past ten years, and because of this she'd convinced herself that breakfast should be nothing more than coffee with the newspaper. So he ate by himself at the kitchen table, cold cereal and orange juice, with an eye on the clock. The Boone home had clocks everywhere, clear evidence of organized people.

Actually, he wasn't completely alone. Beside his chair, his dog ate, too. Judge was a thoroughly mixed mutt whose age and breeding would always be a mystery. Theo had rescued him from near death with a last-second appearance in Animal Court two years earlier, and Judge would always be grateful. He preferred Cheerios, same as Theo, and they ate together in silence every morning.

At 8:00 a.m., Theo rinsed their bowls in the sink, placed the milk and juice back in the fridge, walked to the den, and kissed his mother on the cheek. "Off to school," he said.

"Do you have lunch money?" she asked, the same question five mornings a week.

"Always."

"And your homework is complete?"

"It's perfect, Mom."

"And I'll see you when?"

"I'll stop by the office after school." Theo stopped by the office every day after school, without fail, but Mrs. Boone always asked.

"Be careful," she said. "And remember to smile." The braces on his teeth had now been in place for over two years and Theo wanted desperately to get rid of them. In the meantime, though, his mother continually reminded him to smile and make the world a happier place.

"I'm smiling, Mom."

"Love you, Teddy."

"Love you back."

Theo, still smiling in spite of being called "Teddy," flung his backpack across his shoulders, scratched Judge on the head and said good-bye, then left through the kitchen door. He hopped on his bike and was soon speeding down Mallard Lane, a narrow leafy street in the oldest section of town. He waved at Mr. Nunnery, who was already on his porch and settled in for another long day of watching what little traffic found its way into their neighborhood, and he whisked by Mrs. Goodloe at the curb without speaking because she'd lost her hearing and most of her mind as well. He did smile at her, though, but she did not return the smile. Her teeth were somewhere in the house.

It was early spring and the air was crisp and cool. Theo pedaled quickly, the wind stinging his face. Homeroom was at eight forty and he had important matters before school. He cut through a side street, darted down an alley, dodged some traffic, and ran a stop sign. This was Theo's turf, the route he traveled every day. After four blocks the houses gave way to offices and shops and stores.

The county courthouse was the largest building in downtown Strattenburg (the post office was second, the library third). It sat majestically on the north side of Main Street, halfway between a bridge over the river and a park filled with gazebos and birdbaths and monuments to those killed in wars. Theo loved the courthouse, with its air of authority, and people hustling importantly about, and somber notices and schedules tacked to the bulletin boards. Most of all, Theo loved the courtrooms themselves. There were small ones where more private matters were handled without juries, then there was the main courtroom on the second floor where lawyers battled like gladiators and judges ruled like kings.

At the age of thirteen, Theo was still undecided about his future. One day he dreamed of being a famous trial lawyer, one who handled the biggest cases and never lost before juries. The next day he dreamed of being a great judge, noted for his wisdom and fairness. He went back and forth, changing his mind daily.

The main lobby was already busy on this Monday morning, as if the lawyers and their clients wanted an early start to the week. There was a crowd waiting by the elevator, so Theo raced up two flights of stairs and down the east wing where Family Court was held. His mother was a noted divorce lawyer, one who always represented the wife, and Theo knew this area of the building well. Since divorce trials were decided by judges, juries were not used, and since most judges preferred not to have large groups of spectators observing such sensitive matters, the courtroom was small. By its door, several lawyers huddled importantly, obviously not agreeing on much. Theo searched the hallway, then turned a corner and saw his friend.

She was sitting on one of the old wooden benches, alone, small and frail and nervous. When she saw him she smiled and put a hand over her mouth. Theo hustled over and sat next to her, very closely, knees touching. With any other girl he would have placed himself at least two feet away and prevented any chance of contact.

But April Finnemore was not just any girl. They had started prekindergarten together at the age of four at a nearby church school, and they had been close friends since they could remember. It wasn't a romance; they were too young for that. Theo did not know of a single thirteen-year-old boy in his class who admitted to having a girlfriend. Just the opposite. They wanted nothing to do with them. And the girls felt the same way. Theo had been warned that things would change, and dramatically, but that seemed unlikely.

April was just a friend, and one in a great deal of need at the moment. Her parents were divorcing, and Theo was extremely grateful his mother was not involved with the case.

The divorce was no surprise to anyone who knew the Finnemores. April's father was an eccentric antiques dealer and the drummer for an old rock band that still played in nightclubs and toured for weeks at a time. Her mother raised goats and made goat cheese, which she peddled around town in a converted funeral hearse, painted bright yellow. An ancient spider monkey with gray whiskers rode shotgun and munched on the cheese, which had never sold very well. Mr. Boone had once described the family as "nontraditional," which Theo took to mean downright weird. Both her parents had been arrested on drug charges, though neither had served time.

"Are you okay?" Theo asked.

"No," she said. "I hate being here."

She had an older brother named August and an older sister named March, and both fled the family. August left the day after he graduated from high school. March dropped out at the age of sixteen and left town, leaving April as the only child for her parents to torment. Theo knew all of this because April told him everything. She had to. She needed someone outside of her family to confide in, and Theo was her listener.

"I don't want to live with either one of them," she said. It was a terrible thing to say about one's parents, but Theo understood completely. He despised her parents for the way they treated her. He despised them for the chaos of their lives, for their neglect of April, for their cruelty to her. Theo had a long list of grudges against Mr. and Mrs. Finnemore. He would run away before being forced to live there. He did not know of a single kid in town who'd ever set foot inside the Finnemore home.

The divorce trial was in its third day, and April would soon be called to the witness stand to testify. The judge would ask her the fateful question, "April, which parent do you want to live with?"

And she did not know the answer. She had discussed it for hours with Theo, and she still did not know what to say.

The great question in Theo's mind was, "Why did either parent want custody of April?" Each had neglected her in so many ways. He had heard many stories, but he had never repeated a single one.

"What are you going to say?" he asked.

"I'm telling the judge that I want to live with my aunt Peg in Denver."

"I thought she said no."

"She did."

"Then you can't say that."

"What can I say, Theo?"

"My mother would say that you should choose your mother. I know she's not your first choice, but you don't have a first choice."

"But the judge can do whatever he wants, right?"

"Right. If you were fourteen, you could make a binding decision. At thirteen, the judge will only consider your wishes. According to my mother, this judge almost never awards custody to the father. Play it safe. Go with your mother."

April wore jeans, hiking boots, and a navy sweater. She rarely dressed like a girl, but her gender was never in doubt. She wiped a tear from her cheek, but managed to keep her composure. "Thanks, Theo," she said.

"I wish I could stay."

"And I wish I could go to school."

They both managed a forced laugh. "I'll be thinking about you. Be strong."

"Thanks, Theo."

His favorite judge was the Honorable Henry Gantry, and he entered the great man's outer office at twenty minutes after 8:00 a.m.

"Well, good morning, Theo," Mrs. Hardy said. She was stirring something into her coffee and preparing to begin her work.

"Morning, Mrs. Hardy," Theo said with a smile.

"And to what do we owe this honor?" she asked. She

was not quite as old as Theo's mother, he guessed, and she was very pretty. She was Theo's favorite of all the secretaries in the courthouse. His favorite clerk was Jenny over in Family Court.

"I need to see Judge Gantry," he replied. "Is he in?"

"Well, yes, but he's very busy."

"Please. It'll just take a minute."

She sipped her coffee, then asked, "Does this have anything to do with the big trial tomorrow?"

"Yes, ma'am, it does. I'd like for my Government class to watch the first day of the trial, but I gotta make sure there will be enough seats."

"Oh, I don't know about that, Theo," Mrs. Hardy said, frowning and shaking her head. "We're expecting an overflow crowd. Seating will be tight."

"Can I talk to the judge?"

"How many are in your class?"

"Sixteen. I thought maybe we could sit in the balcony."

She was still frowning as she picked up the phone and pushed a button. She waited for a second, then said, "Yes, Judge, Theodore Boone is here and would like to see you. I told him you are very busy." She listened some more, then put down the phone. "Hurry," she said, pointing to the judge's door.

Seconds later, Theo stood before the biggest desk in town,

a desk covered with all sorts of papers and files and thick binders, a desk that symbolized the enormous power held by Judge Henry Gantry, who, at that moment, was not smiling. In fact, Theo was certain the judge had not cracked a smile since he'd interrupted his work. Theo, though, was pressing hard with a prolonged flash of metal from ear to ear.

"State your case," Judge Gantry said. Theo had heard him issue this command on many occasions. He'd seen lawyers, good lawyers, rise and stutter and search for words while Judge Gantry scowled down from the bench. He wasn't scowling now, nor was he wearing his black robe, but he was still intimidating. As Theo cleared his throat, he saw an unmistakable twinkle in his friend's eye.

"Yes, sir, well, my Government teacher is Mr. Mount, and Mr. Mount thinks we might get approval from the principal for an all-day field trip to watch the opening of the trial tomorrow." Theo paused, took a deep breath, told himself again to speak clearly, slowly, forcefully, like all great trial lawyers. "But, we need guaranteed seats. I was thinking we could sit in the balcony."

"Oh, you were?"

"Yes, sir."

"How many?"

"Sixteen, plus Mr. Mount."

The judge picked up a file, opened it, and began reading

as if he'd suddenly forgotten about Theo standing at attention across the desk. Theo waited for an awkward fifteen seconds. Then the judge abruptly said, "Seventeen seats, front balcony, left side. I'll tell the bailiff to seat you at ten minutes before nine, tomorrow. I expect perfect behavior."

"No problem, sir."

"I'll have Mrs. Hardy e-mail a note to your principal."

"Thanks, Judge."

"You can go now, Theo. Sorry to be so busy."

"No problem, sir."

Theo was scurrying toward the door when the judge said, "Say, Theo. Do you think Mr. Duffy is guilty?"

Theo stopped, turned around and without hesitating responded, "He's presumed innocent."

"Got that. But what's your opinion as to his guilt?"

"I think he did it."

The judge nodded slightly but gave no indication of whether he agreed.

"What about you?" Theo asked.

Finally, a smile. "I'm a fair and impartial referee, Theo. I have no preconceived notions of guilt or innocence."

"That's what I thought you'd say."

"See you tomorrow." Theo cracked the door and hustled out.

Mrs. Hardy was on her feet, hands on hips, staring

down two flustered lawyers who were demanding to see the judge. All three clammed up when Theo walked out of Judge Gantry's office. He smiled at Mrs. Hardy as he walked hurriedly by. "Thanks," he said as he opened the door and disappeared.

# The stakes are higher than ever in . . .

## the abduction

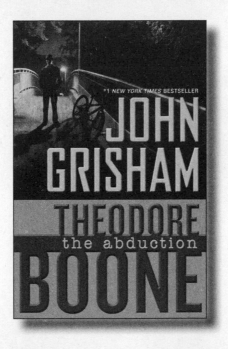

When Theo's best friend, April, disappears from her bedroom in the middle of the night, no one has answers. As fear ripples through Theo's small hometown and the police hit dead ends, it's up to Theo to use his legal knowledge and investigative skills to chase down the truth and save April. Filled with the page-turning suspense that made John Grisham a #1 international bestseller and the undisputed master of the legal thriller, this story of Theodore Boone's trials and triumphs will keep readers guessing until the very end.

The adventure continues in . . .

# the accused

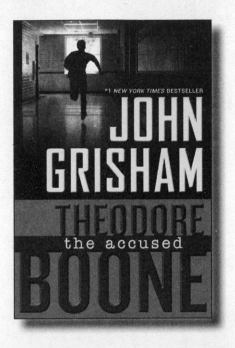

Theo Boone might only be thirteen, but he's already uncovered key evidence in a groundbreaking murder trial and discovered the truth behind his best friend's abduction. Now with the latest unfolding of events in Strattenburg, Theo will face his biggest challenge yet.

**Theo** fights for justice once again in . . .

# the activist

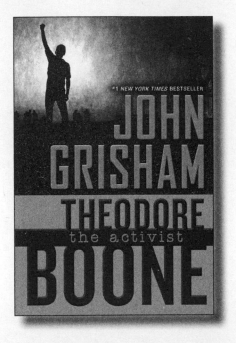

As all of Strattenburg sits divided over a hot political and environmental issue, Theo finds himself in the middle of the battle. The county commission is fighting hard to change the landscape of the town, and Theo is strongly against the plans. When he uncovers corruption beneath the surface, Theo will confront bigger risks than ever to himself and those he loves. But even face-to-face with danger, Theodore Boone will do whatever it takes to stand up for what is right.

**Theodore Boone** thought the danger had passed, but he's about to face off against an old adversary in . . .

# the fugitive

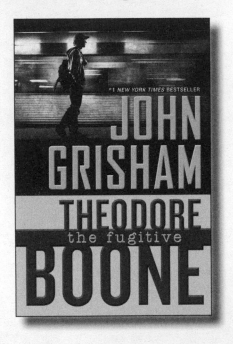

On a field trip to Washington, DC, Theo spots a familiar face on the Metro: accused murderer and fugitive Pete Duffy, who jumped bail and was never seen again. Theo's quick thinking helps bring Duffy back to Strattenburg to stand trial. But now that Duffy knows who he is, Theo is in greater danger than he's ever been in before. Even when everything is on the line, Theodore Boone will stop at nothing to make sure a killer is brought to justice.